Sword of State

The Forging

RICHARD WOODMAN

First published in 2015 by Endeavour Press Ltd.

This edition published in 2019 by Sharpe Books.

ISBN: 9781794611481

CONTENTS

For Pauline

PROEM: THE ENSIGN OF FOOT

30 April 1670

When did a man sense his own destiny?

The question fastened itself in the mind of the young officer of the First Regiment of Foot Guards as he brought up the rear of his detachment in the long procession. To his immediate front marched his messmates, thirteen fellow ensigns in two ranks, the rear of which consisted of Stockman, Fielding, Lloyd, Corbet, Sands, Throgmorton and Razeby. They marched with the utmost solemnity in slow, almost comic deliberation, to the funereal thump of the muffled drums; so slow in fact that Edmund Razeby seemed likely to topple on his spindly shanks, a circumstance sensed by his fellows who suppressed their sniggers amid the hideously overwhelming grandeur of a state funeral. Not one of them had previously seen, let alone participated in, a state funeral. Now they were decked out in obsequious regard for the dead man in whose honour they paraded.

Black baize mourning ribbons fluttered from the shoulders of their scarlet coats; their necks were wound with sable scarves and their large hats decorated with trembling ostrich feathers of the darkest hue. The citizens of London, crammed behind the red and blue lines of the Trained Bands of the County of Middlesex, crowded either side of the gravelled thoroughfare of the Strand. Emanating a faint stink, they gawped wide-eyed at the magnificence of a spectacle the like of which they had not witnessed since the Restoration procession of His Majesty King Charles II, nine years earlier, none of which would have come to pass but for the great Duke whose pompous obsequies they had turned out in their thousands to honour.

Through the thin spring air, above the reverberating thud of the drums, the tolling of the city's half-muffled church bells added to the lugubrious occasion. Momentarily forgetting his military duty, the young ensign who marched with no colleague on either flank threw glances left and right at the pale faces of the smelly populace. Men clasped their hats to their breasts, women blubbered unashamedly, as if they had known and cared about the deceased. The seventeen-year-old sniffed disdainfully at this preposterous display of grief for a man none of these people had known and thought again of the riddle tormenting him: when *did* a man first sense his own destiny? The seriousness of the conundrum acted like a reproof: he faced front, irritated by his lapse in propriety, suddenly punctilious under the eyes of this emotional multitude whose power he sensed as in abrupt realisation. It was such an *immense* novelty, reversing his previous mild contempt, so that he entirely forgot – at least for some moments – the pinching of his borrowed shoes.

Up ahead of him, beyond the dancing pike-heads that gleamed in the sunshine, beyond the ported muskets of the battalion's van-guard, the regimental colours were furled; they too bore long trailing ribbons of black silk, topped by a wreath of laurel. At the very head of the regimental column, leading the slowly trudging companies of musketeers and pikemen as they crunched the specially laid gravel under their feet, marched the battalion's second-in-command, Lieutenant Colonel Edward Grey. Slightly to his right rear came Captain John Downing; both officers bore drawn swords, but reversed, made impotent, tucked under their sword-arms as symbols of deep mourning. The soldier they honoured with such studied magnificence had certainly himself been a man of destiny, of that the young ensign had no doubt.

The young man's eyes flickered again to Razeby's risible legs until the spur's prick of duty made him face front again, mindful of his conspicuous position and that he *must* not appear as ridiculous as Edmund Razeby, borrowed shoes notwithstanding. He diverted his mind, thinking again upon the tormenting question: *when did a man sense his own destiny?*

Was Razeby asking himself this same question? Had such a thought ever occurred to Razeby or any of the other ensigns marching ahead of him? The young man did not know; he did not think the question would arise in the minds of the crowd lining their route of march, for these were shop-keepers, journeymen, tailors, cobblers and men of little account, men encumbered by wives, progeny, the quotidian distractions of making-ends-meet – *ordinary* people. Setting aside the bothersome consideration that he too found it difficult to balance income against expenditure, was it at all possible that such a question occurred *only to him*?

To himself alone? The conviction that this was indeed so stiffened him: but if so then *why*? Why did he, Ensign John Churchill feel … well, something so powerful yet so inchoate?

Because, something whispered in his head, *you are set apart*. The evidence for this elevated point-of-view, his conceit told him, is that you have been chosen to form a rank of your own in the rear of the First Regiment of Foot Guards – all alone under the very eyes of Major William Rolleston, the ten regimental Captains (five of them knights), and its commander, Colonel John Russel, who marched immediately behind him, in the position of regimental honour.

It occurred to the young Ensign Churchill, whose shoes were by now pinching him abominably and the pain of which had now again intruded upon his sensibilities, that perhaps Rolleston or one of the captains, such as Robert Arthur or Sir Thomas Daniel, might be viewing his own calves with the same disdain as he regarded Razeby's. Perhaps he was not so special, after all. Certainly his borrowed footwear confirmed his poverty. (By God, Corbet had such damnably narrow feet!)

Despite the physical discomfort, or perhaps because of it, the question persisted: when *did* a man sense his own destiny? Was this perhaps such a moment? An instant when he was vouchsafed a sudden revelation of the future – *his* future?

Churchill knew that behind Colonel Russel a groom led one of the chargers lately belonging to the dead man to whose good name these excessively expensive and overblown exequies were dedicated. Since they had marched off from Somerset House, wherein the deceased had lain in state, he had heard it whinny intermittently; a soft, gentle sound full it seemed – if one were minded to regard such things as having any meaning – of grief. He supposed a brute beast that had carried a great man upon its back felt something when the great man died, if only relief that the burden had to be borne no more. And the great man had indeed been great; great in girth as well as character and reputation. Indeed, he had been monstrous at the end, bloated with dropsy, unable to sleep lying down and dying as he had been wont to slumber, upright in a chair, surrounded by his officers as if on campaign and holding a council-of-war.

Only one among several of the late Duke's chargers in the lengthy cortege, the softly whinnying stallion was draped in black trappings that brushed the ground, fully caparisoned for war, harnessed and, upon its sable mantle emblazoned the arms of Albemarle – gules a chevron between three lion's heads erased argent. A pair of huge rowel-spurred black glossed boots was incongruously reversed in the silver stirrups. Behind this magnificent steed, whose occasional snicker accompanied a brave toss of its noble head, marched the Lord General's Regiment of Foot Guards. While the young ensign's battalion was commanded by men of impeccable Royalist lineage, having been newly raised nine years earlier at the Restoration of His Blessed Majesty King Charles II, the Lord General's had been a unit of the New Model Army and had served the Commonwealth and Protectorate during the Interregnum. It was, therefore, a Roundhead regiment, but more specifically it had formed the key battalion of the English Army in Scotland, for its colonel and commander had been the great man himself.

Though relegated to the junior position in respect of John Churchill's own regiment, marching behind it, the Lord General's men had been nick-named 'Coldstreamers' and knew themselves to be the older foundation. Symbolically disbanded at the Restoration, laying down their arms in ritual submission upon the order so to do, they had immediately been ordered to pick them up again, resurrected *en masse* into the Lord General's Regiment. No wonder they had taken '*Nihil secundus*' as their motto: second to none. Wondering upon the workings of destiny, Ensign John Churchill could sense them stiff with pride as they too slow-marched, their drums muffled, their officers in black scarves, their colours furled and beribboned in sable. They were commanded by their new Colonel-in-Chief, the Right Honourable William, Earl of Craven, the man appointed by the King to fill the dead Duke's shoes. Craven, it was rumoured, had already received the Royal Assent to rename them the Coldstream Guards later that day.

The sense of the Coldstreamers' pride and pain, their genuine grief and remorse at the death of their Captain-General who they had followed south from the Scottish town on the River Tweed from which they had taken their soubriquet, seemed almost palpable to young Churchill marching ahead of them. He felt somewhat callow, if only for belonging to the parvenu, if senior, regiment. Almost in spite of himself he felt the Coldstreamers' sense of self-importance, generated by the part they had played in the monumental events of the Restoration. He, himself, had been but ten summers old at the time but, unbidden, his back stiffened, he held his head higher and his eyes no longer glanced at Razeby's spindle shanks or wandered towards the staring crowds, or thought of the fluid draining out of his burst blisters to stain and ruin his yet-to-be-paid-for silk stockings. Even Razeby seemed more erect and steadier on his thin legs as the long column with its black mantling, wreaths of laurel, furled colours and muffled drums swung to the left, battalion by battalion, out of the Strand, leaving on their right the reeking stews, tenements, ale-houses and gin-shops of 'Porridge Island' and heading now towards Whitehall Palace and the Abbey church of King Edward the Confessor beyond.

On either side, drawn up at intervals of a fathom, commanded by their gentlemen officers, the Trained Bands stretched left and right. Churchill again allowed his young professional and entirely inexperienced eye, to scan them: citizen soldiers, good for little except keeping their fellows in order, an unblooded and utterly ignorant part, he concluded superciliously, unlike the soldiery of which he was, marching with slow, measured tread to the insistent, rhythmic thud-thud of the melancholy drums. The noise, beaten out nearly simultaneously by the drummers placed every few yards in the long column, thundered back from the house-fronts on either side of the street as they approached the northern entrance to Whitehall Palace.

Here, at the Holbein Gate, the ranks closed inwards for the passage of the portal, slightly slowing the pace of their advance. On his left Churchill had now drawn level with the white splendour of Inigo Jones's Banqueting Hall. This too seemed joined in their mourning, for it was from the black-draped window at the higher end of the building that the King's father had stepped to his execution. King Charles the Martyr many called him, whose death, it was said, had been marked by Almighty God with a new star in the heavens that the astrologers called *Cor Caroli* – the heart of Charles.

The recollection, as they passed the place of horrible execution, almost stopped Churchill in his tracks as his heart skipped a beat: when had the ill-fated King Charles first sensed *his* destiny? Churchill knew that the late King's insistence on his divine right to rule had precipitated his fatal collision with the English Parliament, so where did that leave the question that troubled the young man? They said that even as they tried him for High Treason, Charles Stuart had studiously refused to recognise the court before which he was arraigned. Had he *never sensed* his moment of destiny, or did he deliberately wish to become the martyr of popular belief? The thought was chilling and the young man felt the hairs on the back of his neck prickle with apprehension. Charles, born to be a king, could surely never have sensed he would end his life upon the scaffold like a criminal. And yet he had been condemned and executed, all according to a form of law judged just and satisfactory by those exercising it – all of whom at some time or another had broken their vows of loyalty, just as the great man had done.

Did one sense one's destiny in the making of such difficult decisions, Churchill wondered? Did King Charles not confront his terrible moment of realisation until faced by the full and sombre panoply of a court that, for all his refusal to recognise it, successfully condemned him to die? But that was too late, for all that his stubborn nature lent his hauteur the touch of courage, or was that very lateness, that culmination, the moment in Charles Stuart's life towards which all other moments had been leading?

A man born a prince did not have to consider the quotidian questions of mere survival; perhaps fate made him pay for this privilege by concealing or delaying any moment of revelation. In which case fate ought to be kinder to those with fewer advantages. Surely the hero they were honouring, the Lord-General of all land forces in the Kingdom, a man who had twice governed Scotland, had served Cromwell as a General-at-Sea, who had hoisted his flag as an Admiral under the commission of King Charles II, and stood alongside the King's cousin, Prince Rupert of the Rhine; a man created Duke of Albemarle, Earl of Torrington, Baron Monck of Potheridge, Beauchamp and Teyes, Gentleman of His Majesty's Bed-Chamber, One of the Lords of His Majesty's Most Honourable Privy Council and Knight of the Most Noble Order of the Garter, Lord Lieutenant of Ireland and sometime Member of the Convention Parliament for the County of Devon, a man granted the unique privilege of immediate right of entry to the Royal Presence at any time, a man whom, it was said, the King regarded as a step-father; surely he *must* have sensed a moment of destiny? How else could he possibly have precipitated so momentous and consequential an action as the Restoration of the Monarchy after years of Puritan misrule?

Yet Monck, Albemarle, call him what you will, had changed sides twice! Churchill considered this, concluding, with the naivety of youth, that this had been necessary and – in view of the great man's success – perfectly honourable. His own loyalty was not something Churchill had yet had tested. He was the Duke of York's man, an *élève*, hoisted into his position thanks to the fleshy temptation of his sister Arabella Churchill, the Duke of York's mistress. It was something Churchill preferred not to dwell upon, nurturing his own ambitions and burning to justify his good opinion of himself in the eyes of others. Arabella was but a stepping-stone to him, a means by which he might distinguish himself by his own meritorious conduct. That was why he so ardently sought a sign for himself, searching in the life of George Monck, the first Duke of Albemarle, some evidence that fate showed her favour to those she chose to spring the hinges of history.

It never occurred to him then – such was the callow nature of his young mind which was simultaneously attempting to forget the pain of his pinched feet – that it is not fate that decides a moment of destiny, but the insight, conviction and courage of he who seizes it.

Not knowing that there was no answer to his question, the young officer of the King's Guards gritted his teeth against his discomfort as the procession entered the precincts of Whitehall Palace. The constriction of the thoroughfare increased the thunderous reverberations of the drummers so that the complex of buildings and the long wall to the left behind which lay the Palace gardens, threw back a concatenation of echoes, echo-upon-echo in long and mournful *diminuendo*.

Here it was, Churchill knew, in his official London residence among the Royal Apartments that were commonly called The Cockpit (and which they were just then passing upon their right-hand) that Monck had died upright in his chair. The thought of death, chiming with the exquisite pain in his feet, chilled the young man. A moment or two later they passed the southern King Street gate-way, then inclined to the right and approached the little parish church of St Margaret's nestling in the shadow of the Confessor's great Abbey.

Still the question vexed him.

THE TOWER

Winter 1644

'Sir?' A pause, then again, more sharply: 'Sir?' And again: '*Sir?*'

The young woman stared angrily at the sturdy back of the man in the window. The small stone chamber was ill-lit and his powerfully built body with its broad shoulders shut out what light the gloom of the late November day afforded the sparsely furnished room. He stood stock-still, apparently oblivious to her presence. Aware of his sheer, intimidating bulk, she rounded on the turnkey who stood behind her, her expression a mixture of pique and uncertainty. He shrugged, giving his ring of heavy keys a jerk, which made them jingle, but to no avail; the man at the window seemed detached, insolently oblivious to them both.

'Leave me,' she said in a low voice. The turnkey said nothing but raised an eyebrow. She shook her head. 'I shall be safe enough,' she added sharply.

The man shrugged again, as if absolving himself from whatever befell the silly wench, then shuffled out. As she turned back to the immobile figure at the narrow casement, the young woman heard the key engage the several tumblers in the lock.

'Have you brought my shirts?' The man's tone was peremptory, rude even, but his voice had a soft burr which, despite herself, she thought attractive. He was, she knew, a Devon man, for he had told her so upon a previous visit when he had appeared less offensive. She was disappointed by his present mood of indifference and found herself unexpectedly stung by it.

'I have,' she said, then adding with a calculated insolence of her own '…sir.'

'Please do not call me that,' he said sharply, turning round and confronting her. 'The truth is, I am unable to pay you for your service, mistress, and that grieves me, for you deserve payment.'

She frowned. 'Not pay me?' She frowned fiercely and shook her head. 'Why so?'

'I am out of funds…'

'And I then am out of luck.'

'You are quick with your tongue.'

'I have need to be…'

'What are you called?' He said, interrupting brusquely. 'Did I hear that they call you Nan?' he asked, but did not await a reply, blundering on. 'I do not like Nan, but if you mend my shirts and I owe you money I stand in your debt and must needs call you something … something respectful.'

The sudden mellowing surprised her. The man's tone was still abrupt, but it was no longer unkind and his face bore the hint of a wistful sadness.

'If thou wish it, sir,' she said, strangely mollified, 'please call me Anne.'

'Anne,' he said contemplatively, turning the name over and repeating it. 'Anne … very well, it is a pleasing name, far better than Nan.'

Looking at her properly now, he smiled and his full, heavy-featured face lit up, for it was not only his mouth that smiled, but his blue eyes – and she, in her turn, liked that too. It brought a sense of warmth to her; she had not known such warmth before and, despite the man's formidable appearance, she found that it too pleased her.

'What,' she pleaded, 'shall I call you if not sir? Shall I call you Colonel?'

'Colonel?' He barked a short, self-deprecating laugh. 'No, no, I think not. Not when I stand in debt to you and lie in this place.' He gestured about him at the stone walls and the small, iron-barred window. 'Please call me George as that is the name by which I was baptised … but Anne, Anne, you should not be worrying what you call me when I allow you to darn my worn shirts and then have not the means to give you recompense.' There was a kindness in his address now, and she sensed a hint of genuine shame in his predicament.

'You will pay me when you can … George.' This last tentative, almost shy.

'That is better. Come, sit, if you have a moment to please me further. Have you such a moment, Anne?'

'I have, sir.'

'George,' he corrected.

'George,' she said, colouring and sitting on the rickety chair. She looked down at the adjacent table. It was covered with sheets of paper upon which, it seemed to her, were line upon line of script, *his* script. A quill and inkwell lay to hand.

'That is how I spend my days,' he explained, watching her intently, 'writing.' She remained silent, unsure of what to say, for it seemed a very personal revelation. The act of writing on such a scale as this emphasised the gulf between them. She could both read and write, but never much more than a letter and certainly nothing so obviously prolix. She thought he seemed to sense this, seemed not to expect a response, for he again turned his head and stared out of the window. But then he continued speaking, his tone lower, almost confidential: 'Raleigh wrote when he was here, in The Tower … before King James took his head off for his failure.'

The young woman was not certain who this Raleigh was. Though she had heard the name before, she could not place its significance, let alone the extent of the poor man's failure.

He turned from the window. 'I knew him, you know, when I was a boy. Met him at Sir Lewis Stukeley's … but that is of no interest to you.'

'Is he the man who brought tobacco back from the Virginia colony?' she said, suddenly recollecting what she had heard and eager to show interest in this strange man's past life.

'Yes, the same,' he said, smiling at her again. She was pleased at her contribution to the conversation, pleased that she had not been entirely covered in ignorance. 'And, as a boy, I played with Tom Rolfe …' She shook her head, shrugging. He chuckled. 'No, you would not know, but he was the son of that celebrated Indian Princess, Pocahontas. Have you heard of her, Anne?'

She shook her head again and hung it in shame. 'No, sir,' she said miserably. He stepped towards her and, a finger under her chin, he lifted her head. No-one would ever call her pretty, still less beautiful, but he was attracted by her evenly featured, honest and open face which, though it bore the marks of a visitation of the smallpox, had done so lightly. ''Tis no matter,' he said with a wide smile. 'Truth to tell,' he said, his voice low, reflective and almost intimate, 'I am ignorant too, my education having been cut short by my wilful outrage … so that I was sent away to Cadiz …' His voice faded, he moved away from the young woman and turned again to the window where, for a moment or two, he seemed lost again in his own memories.

She felt confused, unsure whether to be counted ignorant by one who professed the same want of learning – which she did not for a moment believe – or flattered that this important man had reduced his own condition to her own. She held her peace until, after a few moments of abstraction, he spoke again.

'I was born in a house which looked down upon a river, Anne, but not such a crowded ditch as this River of Thames with its fogs and its stinks, but a glorious river that wound itself through wooded hills that were choked with as much game as it was with trout. It marked my father's demesne of Potheridge.' He paused as she hung on his every word.

'Please go on,' she urged him, her voice low.

'My father's family had been lords of the manor since the days of Henry III … seventeen generations father to son and yet …' he sighed, turned back into the room, his left elbow on the window sill and his right hand indicating the papers on the plain table, '… and yet I want the words to do justice to my project which I see you survey with oh-so critical an eye.'

She almost jumped. 'Oh, no, sir, I was not looking! God bless you sir, no!'

He was laughing at her. ''Tis all right, Anne, you may read as much as you like … You *can* read, can you?' he stopped abruptly, then went on. 'I am so sorry; forgive me, I am no gallant as you see, it never occurred to me … can you read?'

She was bright red now, her cheeks scarlet with embarrassment. 'A little, sir,' she whispered. This was not how she was accustomed to behave normally. She was cross with herself, aware that he was playing games with her and yet oddly pleased that he was doing so.

'George,' he reminded her. He suddenly crossed the room, sorted the sheets and then drew one out of the loose pile. 'Here, this seems better written than most. Tell me what you can make of it.'

''Tis getting dark, sir.'

'George. Try, just to please me, though my hand is a scrawl to be sure.'

She took the sheet screwed up her face and her lips began to move.

'Please,' he murmured, encouraging her.

'The … c-a-u-s-e-s …'

'Causes …'

'The causes of all wars may be r-e-d-u-c-e-d … reduced …'

'Good, go on.'

'May be reduced,' she went on with growing confidence, 'to six heads; ambition, avarice, religion, r-e-v-enge, p-r-o … providence and defence.'

'Please d'you go on. Wait, let me strike a light …'

While he struck flint and steel to light a rush-and-tallow dip she rehearsed the next paragraph so that, by the time the flame threw an intimate glow over the paper-strewn table, she had it to her tongue.

'Pray go on.'

'War, the profession of a soldier,' she read obediently, 'is that of all others, which as it confereth most honour upon a man who therein acquitteth himself well, so it draweth the greatest infamy upon him who demeaneth himself ill. For one fault committed can never be repaired, and one causeth the loss of that reputation, which had been thirty years acquiring …'

'Should I, do you think,' he interrupted, 'have written of that single fault that one fault only causeth the loss of reputation, or does it make sense as it is?'

'It makes sense to me …'

'Good. You read that uncommonly well, Anne. And for a moment I thought you unable. You must please forgive me.'

'There is nothing to forgive.' She could not say how flattered she was that he had asked her opinion, whether he meant it or no.

'There is your lack of payment to forgive, Anne, though I promise to pay you as soon as I am in funds. I have written to my elder brother to send me something …' He stopped and she saw that it was his turn to be embarrassed.

'Please,' she said, suddenly softening towards this man who, whatever he had done, deserved her pity for being mewed up in this gloomy place, 'there is no need …'

'Ah! There is every need.' He cast about him, his voice conveying a hint of despair.

'Have you …?' she began but broke off. He recovered himself and looked at her as she sat, her pleasant features soft-lit by the dip, one hand upon the sheet from which she had read as her eyes seemed to rove over his words a second time. He divined her query.

'Have I committed that single fault and thereby lost my reputation; is that what you are thinking?'

She looked up sharply. 'How did you guess?'

He ignored her surprise. ''Tis a moot question, Anne, though I can assure you that I have not yet thrown my good name away.'

'Not *yet*?' she said, her expression quizzical.

'You have quick wits, Anne. No, not yet; though that is what they want me to do, the men in black, to turn my coat and fight against those with whom I lately served and counted my brothers-in-arms.'

'I know nothing about these affairs, but in the present troubles you surely would not be the first.' She spoke firmly, confidently, possessed of good sense and opinion, he noted. That was something to set against her lack of beauty, though he warmed to her pleasant-enough features.

'Do you know of men who fought for the King and then for the Parliament?' There was an unpleasant edge suddenly come into his voice.

'I have heard it said …' She faltered; she was ignorant of politics. Despite the vociferations of many puritan women, such affairs were men's business and none of hers.

'Have you been sent to persuade me, Anne?' he asked, suddenly accusatory, his voice stern. She looked up into his blue eyes and saw in them something terrifying, something hard, like steel, yet cold too, like ice. She shrank back, wondering how she had, no more than a few minutes previously, thought them enchanting. He, perceiving the unintended effect he had had upon her, apologised yet again. 'I did not mean to startle you, but this world is full of tricksters. I would be less than honest if I did not say that I should not much like to discover you were sent to persuade me on the behalf of others.'

'I would never do anything like that, sir. *Never.*'

He softened and put out his hand to touch her bare arm. 'No, I am assured of that now.' He smiled again. 'But I have failed to pay you, and that is reprehensible.' He paused, switching his train of thought. 'Of course,' he said sitting down on the bed so that they conversed more like equals, 'should you yourself marshal an argument that convinced me of the fitness of my accepting a command from the Parliament, then perhaps I might regard it with more charity.'

'That would not be my place, sir.'

'George.' He paused, then asked, 'But how should it not be your place in these days, for now the lowly are raised up and women shout as loud as men?'

'I am not raised up … George … I darn the shirts of those sent here, and they are like you, all gentlemen.' She hesitated and then added, 'There is a bishop here, and another soldier like you.'

'The bishop is Wren, is he not? The late Laudian Bishop of Ely, eh?' She nodded. 'And the soldier is Warren like as not?

She shrugged and he brightened, asking, 'But suppose Anne that you were me, what then would you do? Tell me, for I am otherwise perplexed as I cannot spend the rest of my life here unless the gentlemen in black are minded to send me to meet my maker sooner than he himself intends.'

'You mean God?'

'Quite so. So tell me, what would you do?'

'The Parliament is powerful …'

'Yes; perhaps too powerful … perhaps over-weeningly so and is asking to be cut down.'

'I do not understand.'

He smiled. 'No, why should you? It is of no matter. Tell me, do you speak with all the prisoners at such length?'

'Good Lord, no, sir!' she exclaimed with a hint of outrage, drawing back in her chair so that its legs squeaked on the flagstones.

'No?' he mocked her with a wide smile so that she relaxed. 'I am teasing you. And I would have you call me a friend … your friend George, if you please.'

This reminder of his situation, recalled her own. She recoiled, surprised at where this conversation had led her. 'I cannot do that … George … Damn me,' she snapped suddenly, 'nor should I call you George!' She jumped to her feet.

'Why ever not?' He looked up at her, astonished at her abrupt change of attitude.

'Why sir,' she said, retreating precipitately towards the door, 'I cannot be your friend and still take money for darning your shirts and I cannot call you George because I am a married woman! That is why not and 'tis reason enough!'

She turned, hammered on the door and while she awaited release she lifted his neatly pressed and folded linen from her basket and laid it on the straw seat of the chair. A moment later the lock gave way and the turnkey stood in the doorway.

'Anne!' the prisoner commanded. She stopped on the threshold and turned. 'Come again,' he said, smiling, 'I shall expect you as I should further value your opinion on my book.' He made her a half-bow though she made no curtsey in reply. Then she was gone and the turnkey leaned into the chamber and cast a look about him, staring at the clean shirt as if to see a file poking from its folds.

'Get out!' the prisoner snarled.

The turnkey pulled a face before retreating hurriedly. The door clanged shut, the key turned again in the lock and this time, it being close to curfew, the bolts were shot home.

Colonel George Monck expelled his breath and, alone with his thoughts, faced the long hours of the night.

*

He was at the window before dawn, staring down from his prison-chamber in St Thomas's tower, noting the tide at the flood – the half-flood he guessed – from his elevated position. The tower in which he had been mewed-up, charged with high treason, formed part of Traitor's Gate and from it he watched the shipping in the River of Thames, wishing he was a lad again, looking across the Torridge where it doubled itself like a silver serpent in its meander, and flowed towards its estuary, confluent with the Taw. Had his boyhood been happy? If it had possessed those ancient connections which he had mentioned in passing to Anne, it had not been untroubled. What did it signify if he could trace his lineage through his paternal great-grandmother, Francis Plantagenet, the daughter and co-heiress of Arthur Plantagenet, Lord Lisle, and a bastard of Edward IV? And, moreover, what of a second, more tenuous and tedious blood-line, traceable to that infamous monarch King John?

What did any of that nonsense matter when his poor father, Sir Thomas Monck, was so beset by debt that he was confined upon his own land, encumbered, a prisoner by numerous writs? It was of no earthly account, for Sir Thomas must need send his son George to plead with an under-sheriff that his father might leave his estate in order to pay homage to the King when Charles I made his way through Devon to join ship at Plymouth. The uncomfortable thought stirred Monck from his place at the window. He was chilled and contemplated returning to bed until he realised that his shuddering was as much due to the power of memory as to the miserable, damp and chilly quarters within which he was confined.

He remembered his father's humiliation after he, George, had secured – by means of a little money laid out from Sir Thomas's poor stock – a surety by the word of the under-sheriff Nicholas Battyn, that to honour the King's Majesty Sir Thomas Monck might go unmolested by the law. Alas, his father's debtors had paid the damned attorney more, and the infamous Battyn, having taken Monck's money along with that of his father's enemies, had arrested and imprisoned old Sir Thomas.

In the event, the King by-passed Exeter where the plague then raged, and pressed on for Plymouth, but the sixteen year-old George Monck, disregarding the great power of the sheriff's officers, furious at the deception of Battyn and angry that his father had been betrayed, fleeced, humiliated and confined, armed himself with a sword. Without a word to anyone, he had again made his way into the plague-infested city and gone directly to Battyn's residence. Dragging the under-sheriff into the street, Monck beat him savagely – and carelessly – with the flat of his sword, bending its blade before the wretched Battyn was rescued, cut and bleeding, from the hands of the furiously impetuous youth. Monck was not merely restrained, he was thrown into the city's gaol.

The memory still made Monck sweat, for he had now found himself in serious trouble, locked-up, awaiting trial. Such defiance of a law-officer was an act of high contempt. He might have been hanged for his trouble in defending his father's honour by thrashing a King's officer. He had learned a hard lesson from that intemperate moment, for all that Nicholas Battyn was as corrupt and foul as that other, older, Nick.

Although born at Potheridge in the north of the county in December 1608, George Monck had, of necessity and at an early age, been lodged by his impecunious father with the boy's grandfather, Sir George Smyth of Heavytree near Exeter. Old Smyth, much taken with his young grandson, offered to educate him if the lad lived half the year at Heavytree an offer from his father-in-law that Sir Thomas could not refuse. He let the lad go. This estrangement seemed not to trouble the sturdy George, making him more aware of the name he bore and the family connections he enjoyed. The thin trickle of royal blood was of less significance to the imagination of the boy than more romantic associations of nearer relatives. At Heavytree he was surrounded by uncles, aunts and first and second cousins; besides those that breathed, there were those that had died gloriously. One uncle, Richard, had died a captain; another, Arthur, had been killed in action at the defence of Ostend in 1602, dying at the side of Sir Francis Vere, the first soldier of his age. His great-uncle Francis had sailed with Drake during *El Draco*'s attack on the Portuguese coast in 1589 and had received his mortal wound at the storming of La Coruña. His aunt Grace had married Sir Bevil Grenville, grandson of Sir Richard Grenville who, in the *Revenge*, had died defying the might of fifteen of Spanish galleons in a long and furious fight at Flores in the Azores.

Nor had Monck lied to Anne when he boasted of having known Sir Walter Raleigh, for his Aunt Frances had married Sir Lewis Stukeley, a cousin and friend of Raleigh himself and Sir Walter had called on Stukeley at Farringdon more than once. Besides this splendid acquaintanceship, Stukeley had adopted Pocahontas's son, Tom Rolfe, after the boy's mother had died of smallpox.

Fit, adventurous, bright and eager, all this had led young George to embrace the notion of going a-soldiering, an idea his father encouraged, intending to place him when the time was right. Despite his seemingly carefree existence, however, young George could not fail to be aware of his father's constant indebtedness, not least because the writs against him prevented Sir Thomas from venturing abroad – hence the necessity of seeking assistance from Nicholas Battyn. Thus, when the hot-tempered youth took a sword to the corrupt under-sheriff, he placed himself in grievous danger as the enraged and contused attorney threatened the full and terrible weight of the law. Fortunately the King's intended expedition to Spain was on the eve of departure and, once it was clear that Battyn's greatest hurt was to his self-conceit, George Monck found himself spirited away, attached to another relative, the present Sir Richard Grenville, younger brother to Sir Bevil and grandson of his famous namesake. Sir Richard commanded troops under the able Sir John Burroughs and they were bound upon foreign service. Circumstances rescued the young man from the weight of the law.

As always, when he recalled those distant but vivid and impetuous days of his youth, Monck broke out in cold sweat. But the knowledge as to quite how close he had come to the gallows to save his father's honour, was quickly followed by hot indignation over what had followed. The expedition to Cadiz of 1625 proved the first of a string of disasters in which the hapless young Monck had found himself embroiled. It seemed scarcely credible to him then, in his youthful ignorance, that such an expedition should so miscarry. He understood it better now, but the sense of fury at the waste, the lost opportunities, the useless deaths by disease and poor victuals that had attended the vain and silly operation, still possessed the power to sting his eyes with angry and indignant tears.

For a man of George Monck's imperturbable character, to be so easily moved so long after these events was an indication of how deeply they had affected him. The impact of them was profound, for while he might still sweat at the recollection of his own foolhardy behaviour, the effect of the subsequent military catastrophe in which he had found himself caught-up, still had the power to trigger a sense of outrage.

It had been a tremendous folly. There had been no lack of good commanders – Grenville and Burroughs among them – but the military operation against Cadiz had been appallingly bungled. The soldiers, short of food, had been allowed wine and, in consequence, got out-of-hand. The result had been a humiliating retreat to the ships which, being ill-fitted, found scurvy soon afterwards breaking out among their crews and the embarked troops.

Monck recalled the mood of frustration, the arguments and recriminations among the officers and, perhaps worst of all, the indifference and indiscipline of many of the common soldiers. On the homeward voyage he had much to think on.

This was not the honourable profession of arms his boyhood imagination had conceived it to be; this was a shambles, a national disaster and a dishonourable waste. What had truly shocked him was the change in the greater mass of the troops, for they lacked the heroically steadfast qualities he had thought soldiers naturally possessed; now the evidence was otherwise, for they had demonstrated cowardly behaviour, not the stirring determination that he thought a pre-requisite to the profession of arms. Cowardice in Englishmen was something the lad found hard to stomach, an impugning of an inviolable article of faith akin to blasphemy. But he had witnessed it with his own eyes and the knowledge burdened him, troubling him and lying in his psyche like a curdling of the blood. Those few men who had shown spirit had been in the minority; the rest were drunkards when they could be, or worse when women were available which, mercifully, had not been often on this campaign.

Monck recalled the taint of that return, the taint of shameful military conduct mixed with the taint of his own crime. He had seemed mired in a man's world at odds with his boyhood preconceptions, embedded as they were in family legend and youthful high-hopes. In Monck's absence Battyn had died and Monck had heard it said that the thrashing he had received at the lad's hands had precipitated his death. It was suggested murder might be added to the charges the young Monck had thus far evaded. He did not linger to determine the truth; thoroughly out-of-sorts he left word with Sir Richard of his intentions and fled to London. Although he preferred not to dwell upon those two years of penury and the excoriating dread of being a wanted man, he never forgot them. Most of all Monck grieved for the further trouble he had brought down upon his wretched father's head. It was not what he had intended when he sought out Battyn to chastise him for his infamy.

Impelled by some sense of what his forbears might have done, Monck disappeared, finding in the noise and riot of London an avenue to a quiet retreat, for the Thames was full of shipping. He served for two voyages to the Mediterranean as a gunner aboard the *Perseus*, a merchantman owned by the Levant Company and, in between, went secretly into the West Country to maintain contact with his family. When he heard that King Charles intended supporting the Protestant Huguenots in their rebellion against their King with a new expedition, Monck quietly sought an appointment under Sir Richard Grenville, joining him as Grenville himself again joined Burroughs. At the time Monck entertained no doubts of the success of the expedition. It was inconceivable that it would be a worse disaster than the Cadiz debacle, for it was to be commanded by the foremost courtier of the age, the glittering, glamorous George Villiers, Duke of Buckingham.

Buckingham's expeditions to La Rochelle and the Île de Ré proved even more disastrous than that to Cadiz, but by a feat of arms Monck made his name so that men marked him thereafter. Seeking to rid his kinsman of the taint of Battyn's death by some notable service, Grenville had commended Monck to his commander-in-chief. Entrusted with despatches from Buckingham to the King, Monck's appearance at Court had found a measure of the royal favour. Monck had been sent back to Buckingham with secret information gleaned by King Charles's agents. A French fleet would attempt to cut off the English ships lying in their anchorage and Monck was charged with speedily carrying the warning to Buckingham, a signal honour in itself. Monck had taken ship, but light and contrary winds had held the vessel up, then a foggy calm and the fierce tides on the French coast drove her into a bay where, in desperation, she had been anchored before running aground. Unwilling to submit to further delay, Monck had insisted on being landed by boat and, without a word of French, let alone the *patois* of Brittany, had made his way to La Rochelle, passed through the French lines unmolested, and had walked into Buckingham's headquarters. He had not saved Buckingham from disaster, the Duke would accomplish that on his own account, but he had earned himself a commission as an ensign in Burroughs' regiment for bringing a timely warning.

Now, staring out over the Thames, Monck cast the recollection aside. He never dwelt upon his triumphs, for they failed to offset his sins, but his subsequent adventures in the Low Countries, at the siege of Breda, in Scotland and, above all, commanding troops in Ireland, had taught him much. Privately he considered his experiences to have been a school of adversity which, he thought as his mind ran on to the present moment, had informed the authority with which he wrote his book. He turned from the window to stare at the sheets of his manuscript strewn on the table. In his present predicament it seemed that the only thing he might profitably do was to distil the fruits of those long years of endeavour for the benefit of others. Typically, the thought of those who came after him suffering the same disgrace and dishonour from incompetence and miscarriages, stung him into greater exertion.

Crossing to the chair he sat down and lifted the top-sheet, recalling Anne had read it the evening before. He held it for a second, trying to recapture the pleasure of that moment then, with a self-deprecating shake of his head, he restored it to its proper place among the ordered leaves, drew a plain sheet of paper towards him, dipped his quill and began to write:

He that is a Chief Commander ought to know that if he will be secure in War, he must be watchful and valiant: and that expedition and secrecy crowneth all warlike exploits with success and glory: and that the opportunity of time is the mother of all worthy exploits.

He was back in the stride of the thing now and worked on for several hours, ramming home the hard-won lessons:

War is not capable of a second error; one fault being enough to ruin an Army. It is requisite in a General to mingle love with the severity of his discipline. If thou art called to the dignity of a Commander, dignify thy place by commands: and that thou mayest be the more perfect in commanding others, practice upon thyself. A General shall rule much, if reason rule him and ought to use his best endeavours, to buy good success with extraordinary labour. For industry commandeth fortune and laboursome industry by circumspect and heedful carriage seldom fail, either by hap or cunning, to make good that part, wherein the main point of the matter dependeth. And where the lion's skin will not serve, there let him take part of the fox's to piece it out…

'Aye,' he murmured to himself, 'vigilance and industry, vigilance and industry.'

The key turned in the lock with such an intrusive noise that he turned, almost surprised by his surroundings, so absorbed had he become in his work. The turnkey stood in the doorway and announced, 'The Colonel has a visitor.'

For a moment he thought it Anne, but the gaoler stood aside and he was quickly disabused as a man in the grubby lawn of unwashed canonicals swept into the room.

'I give you a good day, Colonel Monck.'

Monck laid down his quill, scrambled to his feet and gave the cleric a perfunctory nod of the head. 'I was not expecting company,' he remarked curtly, disposing of the usual courtesies.

'So I see, Colonel,' the visitor smiled. His mouth was small, dominated by a long thin nose, his forehead high and his chin pointed. He wore a small, fashionable beard and his own hair. 'And I can see that even if you had, I should have been a disappointment.'

'My Lord Bishop …' Monck shook his head deprecatingly and indicated the bed. 'Pray be seated and tell me …' He paused, turning to the gaoler. 'Get out,' he commanded, remaining silent as the man withdrew and locked them in.

'He will be listening without,' remarked the bishop with a rueful smile. 'There are few secrets in such a place as this.'

'True, my Lord Bishop, but I have little to say to you and therefore concern myself only with what you have to say to me. I see you have not brought me the sacrament.'

'Wouldest you that I had?'

Monck shrugged. 'Perhaps.'

'You are indeed the enigma, Colonel, that they say you are. Tell me, what manner of man art thou?'

Monck held his peace, staring instead at his interlocutor whose identity he knew. Matthew Wren, Bishop of Ely and a

King's man had not visited him out of pastoral charity. Wren knew his man too and, the interrogative hanging between them, waited in turn for the response.

'I am a soldier,' Monck said at last, 'a plain-spoken soldier who knows the value of a stolen march, an ambuscade, the necessity of forage, the provision of sufficient swine's feathers … you comprehend my point?'

'Perfectly, Colonel. But you are a Christian soldier …'

'But not a fanatic, Bishop Wren, for religion, by its arguments and schisms, has provided me with a means of employment and I am myself, not a man given to religious enthusiasms.'

'Yet,' Wren said, gesturing eloquently around the chilly stone chamber, 'it appears you have principles.'

'I hope I have a conscience too,' Monck responded sharply, adding, 'my Lord Bishop, I abhor the means by which men bend the Gospel to their own ends. Religion belongs to God; in the hands of men it has become political, and the ordering of the world is poorly done by it. Were it not for religion, I should be neither a soldier nor a prisoner, but a plain farmer.'

'Wouldest thou obtain thy freedom?'

'What man would not?'

'You could take the oaths demanded of you. I know those who would have you commanding troops in their employ.'

'But you art not of their faction, Bishop Wren, or you would not be my neighbour in this place. You art as bound to King Charles as head of thy church as I am by my commission to serve him.'

'Would you die a martyr for the King?'

Monck gave a cold chuckle and fixed his eyes on Wren's. 'Would you?'

Wren shrugged and smiled, then gestured to the barred window. 'This is a kind of martyrdom, is it not?'

'It is pleasanter than a forced night-march on an empty belly in a rain-storm, to be sure.'

Wren smiled again and nodded. 'Indeed; such things are relative.' He paused, then asked, 'So you place your loyalty to the King above all other obligations?'

'Other than those I owe to God, for I hold the King's commission.'

'And what if the King were cast down in this turbulent time?'

'Then I should serve my poor country, placing that duty above all other earthly demands upon me.'

Wren nodded thoughtfully. 'You are a good man, George Monck, but this is not a time for good men of unsullied principle.'

'I would not have you judge me good or bad, sir,' Monck bristled. 'My principles are simple and soldierly. To him that I have sworn to serve, that oath I must uphold. Should my services be no longer required by His Majesty, I should be free to serve where I wished but, as long as they are …'

'As long?' Wren interrupted. 'The King is not a man to let you go.'

'No; and therein lies the rub of it.'

'So, in the heart of you, you are for the Parliament?'

Monck smiled again. 'Bishop Wren, the Parliament has cast me in this durance vile on a charge of High Treason. It has yet to pass sentence on me, but you know as well as any man, what the awful consequences of such a charge – when pressed – might be. In my heart, and after he who presently employs me and to whom I owe allegiance, I would do right by my country.'

'That is a simple philosophy.'

''Tis complicated enough for the times, my Lord Bishop,' Monck responded with a short, indignant laugh, 'and I do not conceive victory for either party as a simple matter.'

'You have spoken with the King, have you not?'

'At Oxford, yes, as you well know.'

'You have a remarkable reputation for personal courage and skill in war.'

'I have a reputation for luck, my Lord Bishop, and little more. As for skill in war, I learned it in a tough school, as did others who were with me there and who now do prodigious feats of arms.'

'You speak of Thomas Fairfax?'

'Aye, Tom Fairfax and Jacob Astley among others; all of whom are able men, though some let their passions rule their minds.'

'Like Goring?'

'He is not the only one.'

'As you doubtless told the King.'

'My Lord Bishop, what passed between the King and myself was between the King and myself.'

'But you spoke your mind; it is scarce a secret.'

'Is it not? Well, well …' Monck shrugged. 'Well, what other purpose is there in any discourse, but to speak one's mind? That it is rare in this world is a tragedy, the more-so for His Majesty who suffers excessively from want of honesty and candour in those about him. When favour is pursued, the soldier cannot contend with the courtier. Were it not so, I would warrant, His Majesty would not find himself in such a predicament as he presently is. There, my Lord Bishop you have my creed and my reason for placing my desire to serve my country at the heart of my rude philosophy.'

'If I understand your subtlety, Colonel,' Wren responded, 'you hint that the King is in want of thy patriotism.'

'Bishop Wren, didst you seek to disturb my privacy to spring such a trap upon me?' Monck stared coldly at Wren. 'For now I perceive that I must stand charged with treason by both factions in this sorry dispute and it must now hang upon an outcome as to which party prevaileth and may have the privilege of my public and exemplary evisceration! Perhaps, therefore, you will consider yourself a better Christian if you deliver me to that which you represent, eh?' Monck stood up. 'And now, my Lord Bishop, if you will excuse me …'

Wren rose to his feet and held out a temporising hand, motioning Monck to be seated, all the while shaking his head.

'It is true, Colonel, that I am declared for the King and the true religion, why else should I be incarcerated here? But I came as an agent to catechise you, merely out of neighbourliness, thinking that you may desire some society, some conversation. We live in times that would try any man's soul, to be sure, but I do not – and I beg you to believe my word in this, Colonel – I do not come hither to provoke you.' He paused and Monck reseated himself, Wren following his example. He went on, soothing Monck: 'I am myself bereft of any society apart from the intermittent visits of those who have the charge of us and the occasional visitations of the young woman who attends our wants. The truth is, Colonel, I have some books you may wish to read, and access to more …'

'Have you Raleigh?' Monck demanded curtly. 'His *Political Observations* in particular?'

'Why no, but should you wish for a copy I could …'

'Aye, I do.'

'Very well. I see you are working on a manuscript of your own.' Wren indicated the sheets of close-written script.

'Yes.' Monck looked down at his work, embarrassed at the disclosure.

'And I see too that I interrupted you and that your ill-concealed irritation was perfectly natural.' Wren held out his right hand, not for his ring to be kissed, but to shake Monck's. 'I am not a spy, Colonel.'

Monck paused a moment before extending his own hand whereupon Wren pressed Monck's fist and, dropping his voice, added, 'Nor do I particularly wish to be a martyr for the cause in which we two are enmeshed.'

Monck nodded. 'To remain effective, loyalty, like the chain of command my Lord Bishop, must needs be kept simple.'

Wren considered this for a moment. 'Indeed, Colonel, you make a cogent point.' Then he turned for the door and shouted for the turnkey. After his visitor had gone, Monck again addressed his manuscript, reaching for his quill and reading the last lines, to freshen his mind. As his eyes roamed over the exhortation to act like the fox, he cast the quill aside and stood up, returning to the window to stare out over the Thames. Wren's visit had dislocated his train of thought for, in his response to Wren's probing, he had failed to take his own advice; resorting instead to the intemperate behaviour that had – all those years ago – led to him thrashing Nicholas Battyn.

'Too little of the fox,' he murmured in self-admonishment.

*

Two days later Monck was working on his manuscript when Wren called upon him again, beckoning in a woman who served fresh bread, beef pie and cabbage from a covered basket, along with a flask of ale. Monck was disappointed that it was not Anne, whom he was sure had been in St Stephen's Tower the previous day. Owing to his indebtedness to her, he had no cause to expect her charity, but her neglect disappointed him.

'I thought you too busy to dine properly, Colonel,' Wren said with smiling familiarity, aware that Monck was penniless, 'and thought to join you. Besides your dinner I bring you food for thought.' Wren withdrew a book from his sleeves and held it out to Monck, who took it, running his palm down its worn spine.

'Raleigh,' he said smiling. 'I am obliged. Thank you.'

'Come, eat first.' Wren settled himself on the bed, made of it a table and laid out their meal. Monck hesitated a moment, then fell upon the victuals with unmistakable enthusiasm, his ink-stained finger tearing at the bread. Wren watched him, sensing the raw power of the man. He must have eaten like this when on the march but only, Wren judged, after he had seen to his men; of that Wren was certain, without actually knowing why.

'Tell me, Colonel, how came you to be taken prisoner?'

Monck tossed off his pot of ale, gave a discreet belch behind his hand and wiped his mouth with the linen napkin provided.

'I was taken at Nantwich,' he said shortly, as if that were all the explanation necessary.

'How came you to be at Nantwich?' Wren asked, gently prompting him.

'You would that I should relate my history?'

Wren shrugged. 'Only that part which led you to Nantwich.'

Monck considered the request, appreciated the bishop's charity in feeding him, the boredom of their imprisonment and nodded. 'Very well,' he began. 'I saw service under Ormonde in Ireland fighting the Confederate rebels until in September of last year his Lordship negotiated a twelve-month cessation of hostilities in order to bring his army over into England to serve the King against the forces of the Parliament.' Monck paused and stared fixedly at Wren. 'I refused to take the loyal oath that my Lord Ormonde pressed upon his officers under this change of circumstances …'

'Why so?'

'It was unnecessary,' said Monck dismissively. 'And to be asked to do so was an affront …'

'To your sense of honour?'

'Not to my *sense* of it,' Monck responded with a touch of asperity, 'but to my honour itself.'

'I see. Pray do you go on.'

'Please understand the commission under which I served Ormonde was from the King himself, and therefore sufficient to the purpose of the moment.'

'But the Earl's army was being paid by Parliament, surely you can see Ormonde's predicament? He wished to eliminate any conflict of interests in the turmoil of the situation.'

'I commanded the infantry in Ormonde's Army; I was in a position of trust and had held to my charge through considerable difficulties; to have all this service questioned by the demand for an oath of allegiance at this point was dishonourable to myself.' Monck verged on the indignant, regarding Wren as a blockhead. Surely a man who comprehended the mystery of the Holy Trinity could see how the mind of a plain soldier functioned? Monck rammed his point home. 'I am not a man of faction, my Lord Bishop, but a man of principle insofar as this is possible. There is a deal too much made of this oath-taking …'

Monck fixed Wren with that look of cold steel that had so alarmed Anne. Then he shrugged and went on: 'As for the source of my wages, since they were as uncertain as sunshine and rain, my duty was my first concern.'

'And they arrested you for your pains,' Wren remarked with a rueful smile, dismissing Monck's obvious irritation. There was something childish about Monck's still obvious outrage at Ormonde's demand, childish yet attractively honest.

Monck shook his head. 'No, not at once. I was deprived of my command and Harry Warren took over from me.'

'He is here now.'

'Aye, I know, though they will not let me speak with him.'

'I have had the pleasure. He is well enough, and sends to be remembered to you. But how then, had you colloquy with the King at Oxford?'

'Ormonde dismissed me and sent me home on furlough. I was to accompany the army to Chester but word came that the late John Pym had arrived there with the intention of offering me high command in the Parliamentary forces if I persuaded those troops inclined to follow me …'

'That must have been half of Ormonde's force!'

'Perhaps not so many, but the intrigues of Lord Lisle and others, persuaded Lord Ormonde to have me arrested and sent to Bristol. Lisle had had conversation with Lord Digby who had me brought next to Oxford.'

'And what *did* you say to His Majesty?'

Monck shook his head. 'As I told thee before, my Lord Bishop, our discourse was private; besides, I do not recollect precisely what I said, only that I was frank and His Majesty did me the honour of listening to me and then complimenting me upon …' Monck stopped, aware that he had strayed into the Bishop's trap. 'No matter.'

'And Nantwich?' a disappointed Wren prompted, seeking to get at the event by another route.

Monck looked at Wren with a wry smile. 'I observe your sap changes direction, my Lord Bishop, but it will not serve. Still, there is no harm … As for Nantwich, they wished me to go into the West Country but I refused. A civil war is evil enough; to prosecute it against one's native county an abomination. I offered to rejoin the Irish brigade then investing Nantwich under Lord Byron and the day after I arrived, with Warren entreating me to take over, Fairfax struck from out of Yorkshire along the left bank of the River Weaver where four regiments of foot, Warren's included, were in their siege lines …'

Wren was transfixed, watching the professional soldier emerge as Monck conjured his account out of his memory with a spare and impressive imagery that somehow convinced Wren that Monck was incapable of embellishment. He cast aside his precipitate notion of the man's childishness; Monck possessed an enviable and impressive simplicity, straightforward, to-the-point and honest. Wren could almost feel the inspiriting presence of their returned if deposed Colonel reviving men depressed by a siege over a cold Christmas, shivering in their trenches, unpaid and bereft of a commander in whom they had confidence, for Warren was not half the man Monck was.

Monck's eyes now sought the middle-distance of recollection and Wren perceived him standing in the deep snow, pike in hand, as Fairfax's horse trampled through the winter's frozen mantle.

'Hearing of Black Tom's advance,' Monck went on, 'we took up a position about a mile in rear of our lines, formed on Acton church, leaving a guard to hold the place where we had thrown a span over the river. Although much snow lay all about, a sudden thaw had so swollen the Weaver that all the fords seemed impassable and the spate had carried away our own homespun bridge. Nevertheless, we could not risk the garrison attempting a sortie, hence our guard, but our force was now split. With Byron on the Weaver's right bank lay the remainder of the foot and all the horse. The latter, hearing of the alarm, set off to Acton but it took them some time to find anywhere to cross the swollen river and their route proved long, some six miles or so.

'Fairfax was in no such wise inhibited. He drove straight at us, forcing his way through dense hedgerows in spite of the thick and melting snow and was upon us by the time Byron and our horse fell at last upon his rear.' Monck paused and smiled, admiration of his old comrade-in-arms from the Low Countries shining through the recollection of his own defeat. 'But Fairfax faced his rear-ranks about and received Byron's horse on their pikes, then felled them with the muskets mustered in the intervals. It was well done, by God, very well done!' Monck paused a moment, as if to savour Fairfax's professionalism. After a moment's reflection, he took up his tale again.

'Then, leaving three regiments with their fronts reversed, Fairfax drove onwards upon us …' Monck hesitated, his face clouding over so that Wren sensed the agony of that moment as Monck related the dreary sequel. 'Warren's men – *my* men that had lately been – holding the very centre of our line, broke and might have fled but that …'

Wren visualised Monck in his voluntarily subordinate station, pike in hand and raging through the failing and disgraced ranks, *his* ranks, as they sought safety and he roared at them to stand and fight. And yet even now Monck's modesty inhibited him from relating how he had stalled their precipitate retreat, if only for a moment, whereupon Fairfax had broken through the crumbling centre of the Royalist line and torn the wings asunder.

'A moment later the garrison, seeing our troubles, threw planks across our broken bridge, stormed across the river in a bold sortie, drove in our guard and fell upon us from the rear.' Monck relapsed into silence.

'And you?' Wren prompted quietly.

'I?' Monck appeared to awake from a dream. 'I? Why I watched my men run and I saw those that did not run turn their muskets upon the wings which, for a fleeting moment, stood firm.' He seemed to come out of his reminiscent trance and stared at Wren. 'They turned their weapons upon the men that, not half-an-hour since, had stood in the same line of battle as themselves!' Monck's tone was full of contempt. 'I had not seen the like since La Rochelle when I had hoped never to do so again … Men that I had cosseted and loved in Ireland ...'

'Then you were taken …'

'No!' Monck laughed. 'I and a few others, Harry Warren among them, took refuge in Acton Church where the baggage train was parked, hoping Byron's force might come to our aid. After an hour of hesitating, however, Byron withdrew and the church, the train, our artillery, baggage … everything, fell to the enemy. Then was I taken. Two days later my regiment –

my regiment – was enlisted in Fairfax's army and Warren and I found ourselves on our way to Hull, prisoners of the Parliament.' Monck paused again, then emitted a snort. 'Here I was asked to follow the example of my soldiers and repudiate my commission! Upon our refusal Warren and I were sent south, to London here, where we were arraigned before the Bar of the Commons and the charge of High Treason was laid against us. Thereafter, in July last, I became your neighbour, my Lord Bishop, and here I have languished ever since. Now you have a full account of my history up until the present day.'

'And since then?'

'An irregular correspondence with one Cromwell among others, all of whom seek my advice and my participation in forming a new Parliamentary army on the model of that used in the Low Countries. John Desborough came here twice already.' Monck smiled. 'He would amuse you, Bishop Wren, and reminds me of Christ's tempter in the desert. I have agreed that I would accept my liberty only if exchanged by regular cartel. He tells me – Biblical this, and further to your amusement – that His Majesty takes an interest in my case and that officers of the King have several times represented names for exchange, but the Parliamentary Committee of Examinations will not hear of any such thing.'

'They are awaiting your change of heart,' remarked Wren, adding, 'but I fear they misjudge their man, eh, Colonel?'

Monck nodded. 'Perhaps. Desborough claims I am a victim of mine own stubbornness.'

'What said you to that?'

'Huh! That no man was a victim whose honour was intact.'

'Desborough himself might have understood that, Colonel, but the matter is one of politics and others will not.'

'I know nothing of politics, nor have any desire to make good the deficiency.' Monck paused, then eyed Wren shrewdly. He dropped his voice and said: 'If you have the means to carry news to the King, pass word to him to heed what I told him in Christchurch garden.'

'I do not carry news to the King, Colonel. I am incarcerated like yourself ...'

'I may be no politician, Bishop Wren, but as a general field officer in Ireland I appreciate the need of intelligence. Even in this place there are ways and means.'

'You are uncommon touchy about your honour, Colonel,' Wren said, interrupting, his thoughts running elsewhere.

Monck bristled. His brows knit in a frown and Wren glimpsed the implacable nature of the man, sensing the source of his formidable reputation as a soldier. 'Uncommon *touchy*?' Monck snarled. 'How so, sir? How can a man of honour be *touchy* about such a quality?'

'You regard it as an absolute?'

'If by that you mean it must bear the sincerity of …' Monck cast about for a simile comprehensible to a cleric, 'of … of a confession, why of course! What else is it?'

'Many men hold it lighter.'

'Such men are themselves light-weight in proportion.'

'But why so deep ingrained in thy case, Colonel?' Wren suddenly regretted his question for he noticed that, without intending it, it struck deep. He thought for a moment that Monck would ignore it but the shadow passed and Wren saw, or thought he saw, something like relief pass across Monck's features.

'Because, my Lord Bishop, I once did a dishonourable thing.'

'And you wish to make atonement with your *entire* life?'

'Is that not a meet and right Christian thing to do?'

'Why yes … yes, but …' Wren shook his head and smiled at Monck. 'You are unusual, Colonel, and I thank you for your confidence. I wish to God that you had the charge of this country in your hands for I fear the Desboroughs, the Fairfaxes and the Cromwells of this world.'

'You need have no fear of Fairfax, my Lord Bishop, he is at least a man of honour and a damnably good soldier to boot. Of Cromwell and Desborough I know little enough beyond tittle-tattle.'

'Cromwell, I mind, is a man not unlike yourself, Colonel.'

'You know him?'

'I know of him somewhat. He comes from within my diocese and I too have heard tittle-tattle.' Wren paused for a moment's thought, then added, 'Tittle-tattle that speaks of a prodigious, God-fearing man, if not one of mine own mind.'

The two men sat a moment in silence, each digesting the import of their conversation then Wren rose and extended his hand. Monck stood and shook hands. 'Until another day, Colonel.'

When Wren had gone Monck found it again impossible to return to his work. Nor could he sit and read Raleigh's *Political Observations*, though he tried twice to settle to the task. Instead he fell to pacing his chamber, cursing the cold and the ale that had loosened his tongue. He intensely disliked talking about himself, preferring the privacy of his own thoughts, but after months of isolation his conversation with Anne had loosened his guard. Besides, there was something else niggling him, some small spectre that had stirred out of his discourse with the Bishop of Ely and it took him a moment to nail it. He went over the conversation and then recalled the thought, half-formed at the time, but which now struck him with that peculiar alarm that affects those impotent to do anything to remedy an anxiety.

'Cromwell …' he growled to himself. Yes, that was the key to it, Oliver Cromwell of whom he had heard much lately, even here, mewed-up in St Stephen's tower, for Cromwell had ridden out of the eastern counties at the head of a body of fearsome cavalry whose enviable discipline exactly matched the model Monck had pressed upon the King. And under Cromwell, this body of horse had shattered the cream of the Royalist cavalry under Rupert at Marston Moor where, in July last, the Parliamentary army had taken control of the north of England. Though Sir Thomas Fairfax had had the chief command of the Parliament's forces, it was Cromwell and his 'Ironsides' whose crushing rout had swept Rupert's cavalry from the field and clinched the matter. It seemed to Monck that if – and could it be otherwise, he asked himself? – if Cromwell and Fairfax applied the model throughout the forces at Parliament's disposal, that the King's cause was irretrievably lost.

Monck ground his teeth with frustration. Why *had* the King ignored his advice? For all His Majesty's faults – his unreliability, his detachment from reality and his fickleness – he surely must realise that he was fighting for his very life?

The recollection of his encounter with King Charles flooded back to him. He could all but feel the warm afternoon sunshine and smell the grass in Christchurch garden. After his delivery under the tower of Great Tom by a troop of the King's horse, he had been conducted first to Lord Digby, the King's Secretary of State, whose silver-tongue had persuaded Monck to convey to His Majesty every opinion the King sought.

'Having rendered signal service to His Majesty, you stand high in His Majesty's regard, Colonel Monck,' Digby had said persuasively, waving the travel-stained soldier into the sequestered peace of the garden. Seeing them approach, Charles had risen from a wooden bench under a rose arbour, setting aside the book he had been reading. Monck had followed Digby across the lawn, whereupon the King had subjected Monck to that famously seductive smile, almost supressing his stammer as he greeted the man he had once entrusted with a secret message to his commander-in-chief at La Rochelle.

'C-Colonel Monck.'

Monck had bent over the outstretched and elegantly gloved hand. 'I have c-cause, Colonel, to take note of your service yet again, for it was you who saved the guns at Newburn, if I recollect correctly.'

'I had that honour Your Majesty.'

'And got your men safe back to Newcastle in good order, I collect.'

'Aye, sir,' Monck responded briefly, preferring to forget the shambles of the defeat of Lord Conway by the Scots under Alexander Leslie four years earlier. The King seemed unaware of the nature of the humiliating defeat of his forces.

'Come, C-Colonel, w-walk with me. And h-how long were you in the L-Low Countries with the Prince of Orange?'

'Some seven years, Your Majesty.'

'S-seven years.' The figure had clearly impressed the King. 'And you distinguished yourself at the storming of Breda, I am given to understand.'

'I did my duty …'

'And yet you resigned your commission,' the King broke in. 'Pray tell me for what reason?'

'A number of my soldiers misconducted themselves at Dort, sir. I had arraigned them under a court-martial, but the Dutch burgher-masters insisted that I had no authority within their own liberty and that they alone had the power of judgement and condemnation. My appeal to his highness, Prince Frederick Henry, proved ineffectual.'

'A matter of honour, then.'

'A matter of principle, Your Majesty.'

'And not a matter of intemperate outburst, a fit of pique?'

Monck coloured, recalling the rage he had succumbed to at the intransigence of the Dutchmen. 'My men, sir, were my first and only consideration, not only those who stood charged but the effect upon those who did not if I too easily gave up their comrades.'

'And so you came home to see service under Conway in Scotland?' Whatever the King had heard, he brushed the matter aside.

'And afterwards in Ireland under the Earl of Ormonde, sir.'

'Yes, I h-have heard much of that, Colonel, and I have you in my good opinion. For that r-reason I wished to sp-speak with you. P-pray tell me, Colonel, how dost thou see the present conduct of the war?'

Monck, a man of middle height, had looked sharply at the diminutive figure of the King strolling beside him, his cane in hand, his tread measured, his fine featured face with its wisp of beard. The King's seemingly unperturbed demeanour struck Monck as incongruous, even outrageous, had not such a consideration reeked of arrant presumption. The sequestered peace of the enclosed garden seemed a place beyond reality; more a metaphorical statement of the King's position: isolated, remote, detached, disinterested, sweet-scented, far above the quotidian swirl of the wicked world beyond its high and confining walls. For a moment Monck resented Digby's manoeuvring; he himself was a plain-spoken soldier and prided himself on the fact; he was no courtier, capable of counselling a King, and especially not a King so lost to reality. And yet his duty plainly said he must speak. His brain raced as Charles turned and looked up at him expectantly.

'Colonel Monck? I seek thy opinion, sir.' A note of asperity entered the King's tone, 'Be so pleased as to give it.'

Monck seized his opportunity. 'Your Majesty's forces are labouring under great disadvantages,' he began. 'The situation might have been saved after Edgehill and perhaps again, late last year when London lay under some exposure, but the heart of Your Majesty's misfortunes lies with the management of your armies …' Monck paused.

'P-pray do go on.' Charles's interest, if interest there was, seemed affected, a function of Kingship.

'Sir,' Monck seized his moment and plunged in. It was nothing less than his plain duty to speak truth unto power. 'No good can be done with men who have no stomach for the fight for want of pay, victuals and those necessities without which no campaign can be conducted with any hope of success. Want of discipline, so oft attributed to the troops without reference to those who command them, is lacking here too. You have able enough men to command, but they are gentlemen soldiers who see no compulsion to share the hazards of the march, and in that fundamental lack of example the common soldier sees himself demeaned. When all are exposed to sudden shock, it stands self-evident that a body of men needs to conduct itself as one. When the most of it knows its commander and his familiars may bolt upon their horses if things miscarry, they seek not the destruction of the enemy, but the moment of their own exposure. To be truthful, sir, your captains may have no lack of personal courage, but they have great want of experience and firmness.' He paused again, anxious to judge the impact of his words upon the King.

'Go on, Colonel.' Monck sensed he had engaged the King's attention now.

'There is more besides, sir. It doth not encourage a man if he knows that should the shock of battle wound him, he will be abandoned and left like a changeling on the parish. Soldiers, particularly in civil strife, have families and a man lacking in faith in his commanders, fearful for his life, hungry and cold, will think first of his own skin be he given half a chance.

'If, sir, thou wast to set up ten thousand men, picked out of all Your Majesty's forces, and over them commission such officers as were known to have seen service under a general of reputation, who fully understand that an army marches more than it fights, eats more than it discharges from its muskets or its cannon, and wears out shoe-leather and horse-nails at a great rate than it consumes gunpowder and ball, then such men, amenable to just discipline, might achieve much on your behalf. Recall, sir, a force of ten thousand may be paid less than three or four armies each of four or five thousand, yet would be more effectual.

'Forgive me, Your Majesty, but I have seen the state of your troops, sir, and while I do not doubt their professions of loyalty, they are too oft forgot when it comes to push of pike. Moreover, I have seen the like before, sir,' Monck added with an ardent passion that could not fail to catch the King's attention, 'at Cadiz, La Rochelle and Rhé: they are ripe, sir, ripe …'

'By which you m-mean *useless*?' The King had arrested his perambulation, restraining Monck with the merest touch of his cane so that both men turned towards each other.

'By which I do, sir.'

There had followed a long silence and Monck stood stock-still while the King remained immobile, head bowed as he pondered Monck's words. Monck stared at the crown of the King's hat, and the flutter of the long blue-dyed ostrich plume that wound round it and over the wide, encircling brim. Suddenly the King looked up at him.

'Have you anything to add, Colonel?' Charles asked.

'Aye, sir. To press my point, Your Majesty, you *must* adopt such a course of training and superior management on the model of the English brigade in the Prince of Orange's service.

Thus was formed a force of soldiery inured to danger and hardship, watchful over their own interests and calculating in the manner of waging war in which their own lives were at stake. They proved men who were orderly in their violence, calm in the execution of their duty, loyal, brutal – for without force, war was an imbecility – but not vicious. Their rapacity was always subject to the Laws of War under a discipline to which every man subscribed by the contract of his own service. Such an army, sir, would do the least damage to your subjects and their property, carry opinion in Your Majesty's favour where it has fallen away and thus better bear-up your cause to a happy conclusion. Moreover, insofar as it is practicable to do so in any war – but is an objective always to be borne in mind in a civil war – when once the victory is decided between a divided people, all must afterwards live each with the other faction.' Monck paused, then added, 'That is all, Your Majesty.'

The King fixed Monck with his gaze for some moments and Monck, sensible of the protocol, dropped his eyes.

'Look at me, Colonel Monck.' The King's face broke into a smile. 'I thank you for your candour. I will consider your proposal while, in the meantime, my Lord Digby has a commission for you. Go you to Nantwich to which place Lord Byron lays siege.'

Disappointed, deflated, half expecting the King to appoint him on-the-spot to the task of reforming his army so carried away by his advocacy had he become, Monck took his leave with a bow. Digby led him from the garden and the King's presence. As he passed again beneath Great Tom and into the world beyond the yellow court, Monck realised with a shock that the King's detachment was fatal to his cause. Charles's fate was irredeemable.

Recalled yet again to the present, Monck found himself staring down at the filthy Thames as the ebb carried the flotsam of London down to the open sea. The images of the King's smile and of Byron's cavalry wheeling impotently about in the mired snow seen from Acton Church faded, along with the subsiding bitterness that any recollection of his disgraced regiment could conjure. 'And there, at Nantwich, I proved the justice of all my assertions to the King,' he murmured to himself. 'And of what use is righteous indignation?' he asked of himself in a louder voice, turning from the window into the circumscribed world of his small cell.

He took up his seat at the table and drew a clean sheet of paper towards him. Pausing a moment to gather his thoughts, he began to write again.

Men have two ways to come by wisdom, either by their own harms, or other men's miscasualties: And wise men are wont to say (not by chance, nor without reason) that he who will see what shall be, let him consider what hath been: For all things in the world at all times have their very counterpane with the times of old.

He stopped, drawing the previous sheet of script towards him and, realising that what he had just written did not follow, placed it to one side, to be inserted later. It was then that he noticed his stock of paper was almost depleted and that he was about to exhaust the quire that he had purchased. Now he had not the means to buy more and the knowledge robbed him of any desire to write further. After a moment's gloomy reflection he turned instead to Raleigh's *Political Observations*. Opening it at random his eyes fell upon the words:

Whoso desireth to know what will be hereafter, let him think of what is past, for the world hath ever been in a circular revolution; whatsoever is now, was heretofore; and things past or present, are no other than such as shall be again…

A Latin tag followed, incomprehensible to Monck, but the sense of Raleigh's eloquence, so close to his own thoughts, struck him with its coincident certainty. He felt a shiver of something numinous, as if touched by the ineffable.

But Raleigh had been in The Tower too, and his liberation had been by way of the executioner's axe.

*

Bishop Wren became a regular visitor, enjoying more freedom than either Monck or Warren, and Monck began to relax in his company so that their conversation ranged over many subjects. Such was the intensity of their discourse that Monck was reminded of the long conversations he had enjoyed with his old comrade-in-arms, Henry Hexham, the wise and experienced quartermaster of George Goring's regiment in which they had both served in the Low Countries. Monck owed much to the military knowledge imparted by that conscientious and loquacious old soldier. What Monck's precipitate departure from the comforts of home had denied him by way of formal education, Hexham made up for in the speciality of modern warfare. Few understood better, or communicated with more ease, the new and geometrically satisfying theories of pyroballogy accompanying the use of artillery; few could propound with more reason the rules for drilling pike-men and the advantages of the precise placement of musketeers in the intervals between their deployed companies so that each arm complemented and supported the other. Hexham explained the complicated business of siege-works, of mine and counter-mine, of sap and trench, of swine's feathers, fascine and gabion. Most important of all, he impressed upon the young George Monck, was the quartering of men, the securing of their route of march, the laying-in of victuals and fodder as much as powder and shot, all of which knowledge Hexham had acquired as the fruits of long experience under Vere and Goring. More particularly in his influence upon the impressionable and eager Monck, was the impact of Hexham's service. This seemed to Monck to mark Hexham with some inexplicable but enviable virtue, convincing the younger man of the value of experience, of a life of duty in which Monck was able to find himself and throw off the intemperance that had led him into trouble over Battyn. In this way he kept clear of the temptations open to victorious soldiers of fortune and was, in some wise, a Puritan in his profession of arms. When he had spoken to King Charles of men who were calculating in the manner of waging war and orderly in their violence, it had been no conjuring of the ideal out of his imagination. Monck knew such disciplined troops had existed and he saw himself impeccably one of them. For Monck accepted that war was a necessity between states, an ineluctable condition of human existence wherein the mark of civilisation lay in the amelioration provided by the Laws of War. Thus did Henry Hexham have a profound effect upon George Monck, casting the mould into which the ambitious young man poured his very being.

Now Wren complemented the lectures of the old soldier, sensing Monck's desire for knowledge and his capacity for absorbing it, complemented by his unusually serious single-mindedness that combined with an unfashionable disregard for pleasure. Wren recognised in Monck a man of industrious and dedicated temperament, a man who promised – at least as much as such a thing could be expected in this imperfect world – to possess an incorruptible spirit. Shrewdly Wren guessed that that early sin, about which Monck had imparted a hint, had so worked upon him that it had acted as a crucible to the young man's developing character. While Wren knew that Monck could not match the intellectual giants with whom Wren himself had wrestled at Cambridge, especially in that famous disputation of 1616 as to whether a dog might make a syllogism, he knew that those who judged Monck to be dull of wits were wrong, very wrong. Superficially he might convey that impression, but there was more to Monck than met the eye, much, much more. Even in his steadfast refusal to extricate himself from imprisonment, something that had become open gossip in The Tower, Wren saw the working not of a fool, but a deeply principled man. If all men were formed for some earthly purpose, Wren presciently perceived that George Monck had been wrought by God for some mighty work. Monck was, Wren was sure, a man of patience who considered all circumstances before making a decision. And when made, Wren guessed, Monck would act with energetic alacrity, forcing the point with that necessary impetus and force to achieve a successful conclusion. Had he not led the forlorn-hope at Breda, storming the breach in the city's battered walls and thereby decisively carrying the place? Monck had never spoken of it, but Wren had learned the details of it from others, particularly Warren who seemed almost blasphemously close to worshipping his quondam commander.

Although in Wren's intuition lay the envious admiration of the intellectual for the man-of-action, this came with insight and conviction; in Monck, Wren had discovered a man whose services might be indispensable to God and the King.

In prison men find consolation in odd things. Some befriend a rat, others tease the mortar from the stones without any real hope of liberty, others score the resisting stones with their name and the date of their immuring, leaving the fool to saw at his window bars with anything abrasive that came to hand. Wren undertook the gentle mentoring of a spirit he found open to him in the belief that in their country's desperate hour of need, George Monck would prove a faithful redeemer of the King's worthy and righteous cause.

Monck was, of course, quite oblivious to the bishop's adoption of a near-sacred mission. He refused Wren's offers of money, explaining that the arrival of a subvention from his brother was imminent. In fact his most recent and abject letter to his sibling, chiefly exhorting him to arrange for his exchange, yielded neither liberty nor funds. But the days passed until Christmas loomed and on that Holy morning Wren brought him the sacrament, whereupon Monck knelt in humility and received the body and blood of Christ as a Christian gentleman ought to do.

Wren left him on his knees, explaining there were others whose pastoral needs he must attend to.

'Pray give my greetings to Harry Warren, my Lord Bishop,' Monck said to the retreating cleric, rising and turning again to Raleigh's *Political Observations*. Five minutes later he had so lost himself in Raleigh's prose that the opening of the door startled him and he looked up, assailed by the smell of hot food.

'Anne!' Monck jumped to his feet.

'Make some room on the table,' she said brusquely. He quickly removed his papers, allowing the young woman to set her basket down and take off its cover.

'Your Christmas dinner, George,' she said shyly, blushing.

He was speechless then, slavering like a hungry hound before recollecting himself and her married status. 'Madame, I cannot pay thee …'

'Hush!' she insisted, lowering her voice. 'You can, though you know it not. Sit down, sit down, I did not come here on this day to …'

'But what of your husband, Anne?'

'What of my husband? Dost thou want *him* to interfere with our Christmas revels?'

'No but …'

'Then no buts, George. Sit! I command it!' She removed the plug and poured ale from a clay-jug.

'I obey … I obey … But what said you of money?'

'Eat first. Here, this ale is good.' She handed him a brimming pot as if it were a summer picnic, before tearing the leg off a still hot roast fowl and handing it to him. He fell upon it with ravening appetite and they ate for some moments in silence.

'Now, George,' she said at last, wiping her mouth with a napkin and assuming command of the situation, 'I have much to tell you. Four nights ago, towards the hour of curfew, I received a visitor, a gentlemen by his manners and speech, though he would not give me his name. Instead he catechised me mightily and, having done what he thought necessary, gave me this …' She held out a soft leather purse. Monck stared at it; had his brother at last sent him some remittance? 'Come on, George,' she said brusquely, shaking it so that he heard the jingle of coin. 'Take it, for I am full wearied of the charge of it.'

Taking the purse he opened the draw-string and tumbled the contents out upon his rumpled bedding. 'Great God! Gold!'

'One hundred pounds,' Anne said sharply.

'My brother must have …'

'That comes not from your brother, George,' she said, enjoying the mystery.

He looked up at her. 'Then from whom?'

'My visitor, who knew all about you and expressed his regret that you lay in this place, said …' She cleared her throat and her bosom rose with the importance of her task. For a moment Monck thought her a little foolish, until she revealed the source of this sudden wealth. 'Tell Colonel Monck,' she began, intoning the words and thereby betraying that she had learned them by heart, 'that His Majesty wishes him well and much regrets the circumstances of his situation. He thanks the Colonel for his advice, lately given His Majesty at Oxford, and wishes this small sum to compensate the Colonel for the indignity of his present predicament. There, that's all.' She looked at him, pleased that she had delivered the message with which she had been entrusted, as he continued to stare at her in astonishment. 'It's from the King, silly …'

Monck shook himself. Compensation? It was an act of benevolence, to be sure, though he was owed this much and more in arrears of pay. Did this signal His Majesty had taken his advice? Was this a token that his services were appreciated and that even now men were drilling according to his recommendation? If so, why did the message call it compensation for the indignity of his present predicament? No, the King had not taken his advice while the gold, welcome and necessary as it was, was but a bribe.

Anne was staring at him. 'It is from King Charles himself!' she persisted.

He nodded. 'Aye, Anne, I know.'

'Then why do you look like a fool a-staring at the wide open sky?'

He made a gesture with his hands, almost robbed of words. 'I … I am simply amazed,' he dissimulated.

'Well, stop being amazed because now you can pay me.'

'Of course.' He reached for a sovereign and looked up to find her standing before him. 'Is this sufficient for all I owe you?'

She snatched it with a smile. 'It'll do for your shirts and your laundry, and the Lord knows,' she added, nodding at his bed-linen, 'you could do with some more clean sheets. As for your Christmas dinner, that is another matter. I'll settle for nothing less than a kiss.'

*

‘’Twill soon be curfew Anne,’ Monck said later, drawing aside the sheets and pulling on his breeches. ‘’Tis already growing dark,’ he remarked, picking up his doublet, ‘you should get dressed.’ He stood, staring out of the window, allowing her what privacy he could as she too rose from the rumpled bed. ‘The turnkey …’

‘An easy man to settle until his conscience pricks him,’ responded Anne as she rose and ordered her displaced garments, ‘especially upon the birthday of Our Blessed Saviour.’

‘Damn the turnkey, what of your husband?’ he said after a moment.

‘What of him?’

‘You were touchy upon the point last time you came here,’ he said.

‘He married me when I was thirteen and had tired of me before I was twenty. I keep house for him and mind my own business …’

‘Darning shirts for the state’s prisoners …’

‘I am a milliner by trade, sir,’ she said sharply, ‘and my own mistress. I come hither on request of one of the gaolers who is a distant cousin; we thus make a little from it.’

He turned from the window. She was dressed again, and settled her hair as their eyes met. ‘I did not displease you?’

He grinned and held out a hand. ‘No, Anne, you were kindness itself.’ She came towards him and took his hand. He bent and kissed her. ‘I would that we could be thus for longer.’

‘We can be thus for as long as you wish,’ she said simply. ‘I do not do this lightly,’ she added, ‘if that is what you are thinking.’

He nodded. ‘Very well; that is what I wish, for I trust you …’

‘And I you.’

They embraced just as the lock tumbled, the door flew open and the turnkey stood leering in the doorway. Clearly the man’s suborning had its limits and a moment later she had gathered up her basket, whisked up Monck’s soiled shirts and gone.

'Paper!' he called after her. 'Buy me some quarto paper!'

Then the door closed, leaving Monck musing on the remarkable turn events had taken.

IRELAND AND MILFORD HAVEN

Summer 1646 – Summer 1649

'Get up!' The turnkey grinned, enjoying the discomfiture caused to the prisoner by the stridency of his command. It was not often that he caught Colonel Monck at a disadvantage. 'The Governor will see thee shortly.'

'Keep a civil tongue in thy head,' a frowning Monck said, swinging his legs out of bed. 'And bring me a decent breakfast, you damned rogue.'

'Only if I see the colour of thy money …'

Monck reached under his pillow for his purse. 'There's tuppence,' he tossed the coins at the wretched man. 'Now get out and learn to respect thy betters.'

Muttering that money did not make a gentleman the turnkey left Monck to tuck his purse away. In turn Monck was thankful that Anne supplied him with small coin, enabling him to outflank the roguish gaoler in his constant campaign to fleece his charges. He smiled as he recollected hearing her remonstrating with the turnkey over his charges, feeling profoundly grateful to her for all the services, great and little, personal and general, that she had rendered him in the eighteen months following that Christmas when they had first become lovers. Ever since she had come to him regularly, providing him with goose-quills, ink and paper, clean sheets and new clothes when he asked her as he eked out the King's bounty.

Having shaved, Monck put on his best doublet, thinking of the news that Anne had brought him of events beyond the confining ramparts of the fortress, news not perhaps unconnected with the Governor's summons. As the clock of nearby All Hallows struck nine, purposeful footsteps sounded outside his cell; a moment later the door flew open and the turnkey stood deferentially aside.

Since the Parliament's ruling Council of State had fully garrisoned The Tower, Sir Robert Harley had enjoyed the luxury of being largely its Governor *in absentia*. However, his attendances had been increasingly marked ever since that April, when Parliament had ordered a return to be submitted of all imprisoned soldiers-of-fortune who might be willing to serve the Parliament abroad. Monck had received one earlier visit and had returned the same answer that he had made constantly: that he would do nothing to compromise his oath or his commission. For the meanwhile he therefore continued in his cell, an increasing embarrassment and burden to his captors. Notwithstanding this intransigency, he received more visitors, including the young Philip Sydney, heir to the Earl of Leicester, who now enjoyed the courtesy title of Lord Lisle. Lisle seemed anxious to pick Monck's brains on military operations in Ireland while simultaneously attempting to coerce him to submit to the demands of Parliament.

But that sunny June morning of 1646 Sir Robert Harley came to him with news of a different kidney and, as each bowed to the other, Monck knew his instinct had been correct.

'Colonel Monck,' Harley said inconsequentially, with a pleasant smile as he straightened up and acknowledged Monck's courtesy in indicating he should occupy the worn chair by his table.

'You have news, I think, Sir Robert,' Monck said expectantly, as Harley eased himself onto the creaking seat.

'I have indeed. You will have heard, no doubt, that the King's fortunes have sunk so low that he has given himself up to the Scots.'

Monck nodded. 'Yes, that much I had heard.'

'I am in consequence charged to offer you the taking of the negative oath. Should you formally apply to do so – and the act must, of necessity, come from you – your services will be employed abroad …'

'In Ireland?' Monck broke in.

Harley made a gesture suggesting that this was likely, then asked: 'Does this not relieve you of your misgivings? I am charged privately to suggest to you that you would be made most welcome in the Parliament's service.'

'So Lord Lisle had been insisting.' Monck paused a moment, then added: 'I seek only to serve my country, Sir Robert.'

'Colonel Monck …' Harley began, a hint of exasperation in his voice, but Monck cut him short.

'Sir Robert,' he said curtly, 'please convey to those who sent you my desire to be of service to the Kingdom.'

Harley looked taken aback, as though he had anticipated a long argument with this dull and obdurate man whose skills – so they said – were of prime importance to those charged with the suppression of the Irish rebels. He stood up, gesturing to the ink and paper on the table. 'If you would make an application now, I should be pleased to carry it thither.' He made way for Monck, who took the seat, drew a blank sheet of paper towards him and trimmed his quill. 'You will be required to leave the country within a month, Colonel …'

Monck looked up at Harley. 'A month … very well.' Then, oblivious to Harley's look of mild contempt, he bent to his task. Watching Monck, Harley concluded those who wished Monck deployed in Ireland knew what they were doing. Few emerged from that unhappy island with a reputation to be proud of; Monck was just the man to do his worst and carry off the opprobrium, sparing the Parliament's other military officers for the more important business of securing England and dealing with the vexing problem of King Charles and the Scots. A moment later Monck shook the paper, drying the ink, before handing it to the waiting Governor. 'It is good of you to wait, Sir Robert.'

Imbued as he was with a slight prejudice against the prisoner, Harley missed the irony in Monck's tone. 'It is good of you to act so promptly, Colonel,' Harley replied with a courteous relief now his mission was accomplished, though he ran his eyes rapidly over Monck's neat script. Looking up he smiled. 'This will do splendidly, Colonel. I hope in a few days, perhaps a week …'

'Yes, yes, Sir Robert,' Monck responded and Harley felt himself dismissed, puzzled by an odd sensation of inferiority

Monck had suddenly – and quite unavoidably – imposed upon him. Recovering himself, Harley explained that until a formal response was received he was bound to maintain Monck as a prisoner. Monck simply bowed, a gesture Harley uncomfortably felt, was redolent of condescending acquiescence.

Left to himself Monck's thoughts were complicated. Almost entirely institutionalised, he felt a fluttering of misgiving at the prospect of liberation, not least because it ended his long and stimulating discourses with Wren. Most of all he was troubled at the loss of Anne's company, but these fears soon evaporated and, suddenly resolute, he banged on the door, shouting for the turnkey who, when he arrived red-faced and abusive, was swiftly silenced.

'Do you pass word to Mistress Ratsford that I would fain have all my shirts back instanter and,' he rummaged for the purse, 'here's for your trouble.'

The turnkey stared down at the farthing. 'Is this all?'

'That is all for now,' Monck snarled. 'Now do as you are bid!'

Anne was with him next morning and he broke the news to her. 'I am to be out of the country within a month, my dear, but much of that I shall need to ready myself as I have little enough in the way of equipage …'

'Of course, of course,' she said, her eyes filling with tears.

'Listen to me Anne,' he said, turning to her and addressing her with a sudden insistence. 'If all goes well, I shall not forget you. That I promise you upon my word of honour. I have still a small sum and shall press most of this upon you when I leave, so make certain you are in daily contact, for I do not yet know the date of my release and it may be sudden.'

She nodded, though the tears now flowed down her cheeks so that he put a finger under her chin and raised her face. 'Come, Anne, come; surely you would not see me mewed up here for my entire life?'

She did not answer him directly, saying: 'These past months have been the happiest of my life …'

He stared at her for some moments, as if assimilating the import of this simple and disarming statement. Then he nodded abruptly. 'Cleave to my memory, Anne, and, when the wheel of fortune hath spun a little we may yet bring this matter between us to a conclusion satisfactory to us both.'

'You would have me …?' she said uncertainly.

'With, or without the encumbrance of a husband, if *you* will have *me*.'

'I swear it,' she said intensely.

'So then do I, but we must perforce wait upon events.'

They embraced passionately and Monck drew her towards the bed. She demurred, pleading her lunar intervals were upon her, but promising that, if it were possible, they should share a bed before he left London.

'Very well,' he smiled, turning to his table where, neatly piled and tied with string lay the treatise upon which he had laboured for so long. 'There is one thing beside the money, Anne, I would pass these papers into your safe-keeping, for I cannot carry them on campaign and I have long since completed my argument therein. Shall you do that for me?'

'Of course, George, though I shall be troubled by the responsibility.'

'Let that be a further earnest of our continuing association.' He smiled at her and she saw again the bright sparkle in his blue eyes.

*

Hearing of Monck's imminent release through the turnkey, Bishop Wren paid him a last visit, wishing him well.

'Thank you,' Monck said simply, and Wren detected a change in the man, as though the prospect of liberty imbued Monck with a sudden, startling energy. It was not to be wondered at, Wren concluded, contemplating his own less certain future.

'Shakespeare, in *Julius Caesar*, speaks of there being a tide in the affairs of men that, taken at the flood, leads on to fortune, Colonel. I am persuaded that such a tide is now upon the make, at least in your own case.'

'I am unfamiliar with the Bard, my Lord Bishop, despite all your wise counsel in these past months,' Monck said smiling.

'Well, well; no matter. Now at least you have your wish, to serve the state.' Monck nodded. 'And shall you serve the King?' Wren added.

Monck looked squarely at Wren. 'You know my mind well enough. I shall do that service that lies in my power and inclines for the betterment of the country. Much may yet depend upon the King, but in their New Model Army the Parliament has a weapon of far superior steel to anything coming readily to the King's hand.'

'Well, he is in the hands of Scots now and they are, I hear, likely to open negotiations to deliver him up if Parliament indemnifies them for the expense of the late war.' Wren paused. 'There is hope that the King may come round and accept a compromise …'

'Never!' Monck shook his head vehemently. 'The King may say such a thing but I do not for an instant believe he will submit.'

Wren considered Monck's reply then shrugged. 'It may be the worse for all of us if he does not find some accommodation …'

'Mercifully,' Monck said abruptly, 'I am free of such politics.'

Wren accepted the change of subject. 'Shall you command in this new army, do you know?'

'I doubt it; if I am intended for Ireland I shall command a rag-bag of the old Irish regiments and be expected to perform wonders. I must take my chance but at least it is employment. Fairfax will hold the prime force in England and much will depend upon what commission I am given.'

'Let us hope they make you a commander-in-chief,' Wren said encouragingly.

'Huh!' Monck laughed at Wren's military naivety, 'I doubt they will do that, my Lord Bishop. Remember, I am still an unknown quantity, untested in the service of my new masters …'

'Not unknown, Colonel, or you would not have been so favoured. Besides, I know your men call you Honest George.'

'You know too much, Bishop,' Monck riposted, blushing furiously.

*

'Oaths! Oaths! If a war was to be won by the swearing of oaths we should have no end of victories and want a new war to swear them to! No, my Lord, I shall not take another oath beyond that directly pertaining to my commission. As for taking the Covenant, that I will not do.'

The twenty-seven year-old Lord Lisle stared at the man before him, noting the leaner face and paler skin that, more visible in a better light, were the products of his long imprisonment. 'You do not change, Colonel,' he said with a sigh.

'You would not have summoned me if I had,' Monck retorted shortly, aware that his intransigence embarrassed the inexperienced Lisle. A member of the ruling Parliamentary Council of State that sat at Derby House, Lisle had summoned Colonel Monck to a meeting to sound him out for service in Ireland where, in the eyes of the Derby House Committee, the situation had become intolerable.

Ireland had languished under a partial peace since the time of Ormonde's composition with the rebels. This had released the English troops in Ireland for service at home, for Ormonde had had no powers to treat on behalf of the Scots forces in Ulster. Since the end of the Civil War in England, the victorious English Parliament was eager to bring the Irish to heel and avenge the spilling of Protestant blood in their unhappy land. With the Protestant Ulster Scots of Parliament's opinion, if not quite at its side, Dublin and most of Leinster was still held by Ormonde in the name of the King. In the south Lord Inchiquin had come over to the Parliament and, adopting a Parliamentary title, sought to rule Munster in its name. As for the rest of the country, it was held in loose confederation by the Papal Nuncio, Giovanni Battista Rinunccini, Bishop of Fermo, who – having arrived with a war chest, swords, pike heads, several thousand stand of arms and ten tons of gunpowder – had set up his headquarters in Kilkenny. From here he had formed a Catholic party by uniting the recusant Catholic 'Old English,' under Colonel Thomas Preston, with the Gaelic tribes under Owen Roe O'Neill. Rinunccini nursed the pious objective of placing the province thus created under the protection of Spain and holding it in the name of the Pope. This was incendiary to the sober-suited men of Derby House.

As Monck emerged from The Tower and prepared to go on campaign, the agents of Parliament sought to prevent Inchiquin, a man given to consequential fits of pique, again changing sides and joining Ormonde. In the Commons the members argued about who was best fitted to act as Lord Lieutenant and command the forces being mustered to embark for Ireland. In the meanwhile Ormonde, now pressed by the rebels and retiring within the Pale, offered to surrender Dublin to Parliament rather than allow the Catholic party a victory. Significantly, Ormonde urged upon the Parliament a recommendation to send out Colonel Monck and those officers of the Irish brigade whom Monck favoured, including Harry Warren, who had gone into England with him. Parliament, anxious that Inchiquin would change sides yet again if Dublin fell to the Catholics, finally decided upon Lisle, as Lord Lieutenant. The complications of competing factions, particularly among the Presbyterians who were, in theory, Royalist, welcomed Ormonde's advice while Lisle, eager to find some competent military officers capable of delivering the cause from this morass, thus found the wind blowing in George Monck's favour. To find the man himself unwilling to undertake a role he was fitted for and, in all other respects, eager to embrace, all upon account of an oath, seemed the very pinnacle of perversity. But he knew Monck better than to remonstrate further.

Instead he smote his thigh with exasperation. 'I wash my hands of you, Colonel,' he said. 'The Irish Committee of the Council of State will want to see you and you may lay your case before them but I warn you, the Presbyterians among us will insist upon your taking the Covenant.'

'We shall see, my Lord,' Monck answered shortly.

'Tomorrow, then,' Lisle said, waving his dismissal. Monck bowed and withdrew.

The following day Monck emerged from his encounter with the Irish Committee; he had persisted in his refusal to take the Covenant, though the Committee reported to the House of Commons that he had done so, thus securing both his services and his freedom. Later, just before he left London, he confided to Anne Ratsford that he had agreed only to hold his commission as others did.

''Twas a form of words with which they had to be content. It meant to each that which he desired, and only one – a Presbyterian! – objected.'

It was now autumn and, despite protestations of urgency, Lisle's orders were not forthcoming. Delay followed delay as first Ormonde and the Parliamentary Commissioners sent to Dublin to treat with him argued over the terms of the surrender, and then at home the difficulties of raising three and a half thousand foot and six hundred horse met obstacle after obstacle. It was late February of 1647 before Lisle, with Monck in his train, landed his forces in Ireland, not at Dublin, but at Cork where Lisle was immediately embroiled in further arguments with Inchiquin, a vain man of similar age to Lisle. Owing to his own youth and inexperience, the term of Lisle's commission had been limited; by now it had only a few weeks to run. By the time of its expiry in April not a thing had been achieved and by May Day Monck found himself back in London.

'I seem,' he said to Anne, with an air of weary resignation, 'to be destined always to be attached to military failure.'

But two months later the wheel of fortune turned again and a messenger knocked at his lodgings, summoning him to appear once more before the Irish Committee. He returned four hours later and sent word for Anne to come to him when she could. That night he told her of his appointment as Sergeant Major General of the Scots and English forces in the counties of Down and Antrim. She listened patiently though uncomprehending as the flood of words poured from him, an oddity coming from a man she knew to possess a reputation for grim taciturnity. Ignorant of the meaning of this tumbling discourse, she was intuitively aware that he had need of her ear, and that this unpredictable animation was a product of his frustrating years of incarceration and unfulfilled ambition. What she could not know was that George Monck was outlining the strategic position and applying the observed principles which he had so carefully laid down in his manuscript.

The only thing Anne understood was that the Marquess of Ormonde had quit Ireland in late July, handing his forces over to Colonel Michael Jones, a Protestant officer, and that Oliver Cromwell had been instrumental in persuading the Council of State to abolish the role of Lord Lieutenant and leave Michael Jones and George Monck to destroy the rebels.

'Mark my words, Anne, if Jones and I cannot finish the business, Oliver Cromwell is itching to campaign against the Catholics. In the meanwhile Jones is to have Leinster and I, with seven thousand pounds, am to command Ulster.'

'Seven thousand pounds?' said an astonished Anne, for whom the sum seemed impossible.

'Aye, in my charge as is my money in thine.'

*

'Lord, how a man must dissemble just to keep his feet in this benighted land!' Monck exploded so that his assembled staff, their faces long and woeful, regarded their chief with a mixture of suspicion and dread. Honest George, they felt, had not proved honest enough and his army, short of food and powder, was dismayed to learn their commander had been treating with the rebel O'Neill, offering him six barrels of gunpowder as the price for a cessation of hostilities. Monck stared about him, glaring at the assembled officers one at a time. Not one of them met his gaze. He knew their opinion of him and cared not a fig for it.

'What is the temper of the men?' he growled. There was an awkward silence. 'I asked a question, gentlemen.' Monck's tone was menacing.

'Sir, if I may …'

'No sir! You may not; what is the temper of the men?'

'They are unhappy, sir … the situation as revealed by this matter of Colonel Ferral ...'

'Very well; it may surprise you to know that I understand their anxiety, that I sympathise with their position but …' he paused for emphasis, 'but, let me make it quite clear that I command and that I charge you, as you have sworn your obedience so to do, that at the first whiff of sedition or mutiny you shall inform me of it directly.' They were looking at him now. This was no round-robin diatribe but an order issued to each and every one of them. He met their gaze, fixing each of them with his implacable eye.

'Very well; that is all.'

'Damn Ferral!' he muttered as he relieved himself of baldric and sword, calling for his man-servant to divest him of his cuirass. He had ridden through the lines of the encampment that morning and noted for himself the resentment, anger and, often-enough, mere incomprehension that marked the men's faces as they broke their fasts and went about their chores. He heard too, their mumbling opinion offered to his back. God knows they were a small enough force to hold down this wretched country, but he – and they – had done his best. Had it not been for the incompetence of Ferral in holding his men in check at Dundalk … but it was done now. Done, and, with Inchiquin in the know, and Parliament next to be informed, Monck knew the matter would see him damned. He was furious for having been caught in a political trap, a victim of secret orders. But it was no good dwelling on that. He cursed again; such was his sense of responsibility that he was, in any case, incapable of passing the blame; besides, at the time he had been happy enough to fulfil the instructions he had received by the hand of an officer from England. The red coats of the newcomer's escort and his own sash had proclaimed him a squadron commander of one of the New Model Army's cavalry regiments. So conspicuous an arrival had been announced as despatches from the Council of State and Monck had been handed a General Order to the Army in Ireland. Besides this, however, Captain Arthur had brought a secret communication for Monck's eyes only and Monck knew the signatory of the sealed letter.

But the gunpowder had been an error; a mistake, he feared, as consequential as his youthful assault on Nicholas Battyn. Monck caught himself from too excoriating a self-condemnation. The assault on Battyn had been wild and intemperate, a furious and emotional response to his father's deep and public humiliation as much as a young man's judgement on an older man's venality. The gunpowder for O'Neill had been a calculation, a calculation necessary to clinch a deal, it was true to say, for Monck knew that O'Neill's demands were so outrageous that, while his secret instructions insisted he immobilised O'Neill in arranging an accommodation, the rebel chief's conditional demands and any armistice that went with them, would be rejected. With ratification impossible and his secret instructions explicit, Monck had to play for time he did not have, so succumbed to the ploy of passing the gunpowder and a quantity of ammunition to the enemy by way of a circumvention. He knew that once he had the powder in his possession O'Neill would again enter the field if his demands were not met, but those six barrels were intended to persuade the Irish commander that Monck at least was to be depended upon – at least as long as he commanded in Ulster. If only Ferral's men had not over-steeped themselves in drink in Dundalk and blown the ploy to Kingdom Come, God rot them!

O'Neill had sent Colonel Ferral and five hundred men to collect the powder but they came upon quantities of liquor in Dundalk and, on their way home with their prize, they were ambushed by Inchiquin who, informed of the treachery, cut them to pieces and exposed Monck's part in the affair.

Matters began well enough, he wrote to Anne in August of 1649, the first letter she had received since his departure two years earlier. *Preston was soon dealt with*, he went on, referring briefly to the routs inflicted on the rebels at Dungans Hill and Knocknanaus, *but O'Neill and his wild Irish proved a more intractable problem*. O'Neill, he explained briefly, was an old Low Countries warrior, dogged, redoubtable and long experienced in the Spanish service, who had taken to waging partisan warfare. Barely comprehending the words that she made out with difficulty, reading them as she did in her small bed-chamber, one ear cocked in case her husband returned, she was overwhelmed with a sense of connection with her lover despite the long break in their communication. Like that outpouring of words on the eve of his departure, this letter was evidence of the great confidence he placed in her and she felt an obligation to struggle to the end of his missive. Hoping she would not be disturbed, she read on.

We met him at his own game, scouring the glens of Antrim, burning, ravaging and plundering for provisions, of which we are always in want. The renewal of the Civil War in England so curtailed all the support of which we had expectation from home, that we were obliged to depend upon our own resources. Even so, we so reduced much of Ulster to a governable state that I flatter myself to say the country was quiet and showed even a tendency to prosperity. So severe had our chastisement proved that I received offers of information, appointing a Scout-Master to garner intelligence and, in this wise, any raid O'Neill contemplated was met in the moment of its execution and scattered like dust along the highway.

In digging their own potatoes in land once possessed by O'Neill's ragamuffins, my soldiers' prosperity was the ruin of O'Neill's men and I came less-and-less to rely upon supplies from England. Finding it unnecessary to harry a man no more than the prosecution of successful war demanded, some at least of those set against us began to weaken. By mingling love with severity of discipline I hoped to persuade them to lay down their arms and to come in to us. Alas, it was never to be, far too many were at the game in their own interest and all the while there was such turmoil in England that we began to feel forgotten.

The troubles that now assailed us were endless, turbulent and, like a great wave of the sea, overwhelming. Ormonde's intrigues with the Scots Presbyterians bore fruit in Ireland as well as England. In the south Inchiquin went over to Ormonde and the King, whereupon Munster was lost to the Parliament just as the new war broke out in England. All was now confusion as Inchiquin sought alliance with the Scots settlers in Ulster. These were divided among themselves but, seeing the danger most in my rear, with Munro and his once loyal Scotchmen in Belfast and Carrickfergus, I hurried to his headquarters with a body of men and took him. He has since been committed to The Tower and I made Governor of Belfast with five hundred pounds to my credit. With the news of General Cromwell's victory over the Scots at Preston, we looked for better times, unknowing that matters lay unresolved in England between the Presbyterians and the Independents in Parliament, and all in expectation of reinforcement of a grand expedition to Ireland. Then came the news of the King's trial and execution…

Anne laid the letter down. There were still several pages to read but while she found Monck's account incomprehensible, the reference to the execution of King Charles at the end of January last, brought the reality of these events vividly to her imagination. The King's execution had touched London – and herself – directly.

She remembered that cold January day, with the City streets empty as if a sluice had been opened and all those who normally crowded its narrow thoroughfares had been carried westwards by a relentless tide of curiosity, to crowd Whitehall and gawp at the awful and sombre spectacle. She had not taken much interest in the King's arrest and knew only that he seemed to her uneducated and ill-informed perception, a man incapable of settling to his divinely ordained task. To her the art of kingship seemed a simple matter: just as, in often impossible circumstances, she ran her small household and modest business tending the state's prisoners in The Tower and making an occasional bonnet, it seemed all a king had to do was keep his people happy. How Charles had so signally failed to accomplish this was a mystery past her divining, but it seemed – from what little she knew – that he never kept his word and never listened to advice. That he was brought to a trial was less of a shock than the news that he was to be executed.

'Could he not be imprisoned?' she had asked her husband when he was expatiating upon the day's events in the court then trying him as they were being gossiped about in every tavern and alehouse in London.

'Nah!' Ratsford had expostulated, treating his young wife – unusually enough – to a malodourous and carried smile. Warmed with ale and the pleasing prospect of one of the world's great being brought low, Ratsford felt uncommon stirrings in respect of the woman bustling about her kitchen. 'E's too slippery,' he declaimed with a superior air, 'can't be trusted an' got too many friends as wants ter make trouble, like. Better for me an' you that he's done away with, sent to the Devil in two parts …' He laughed at his own wit.

'But what will become of the country with no King?'

'We'll still 'ave a bloody Parliament! Strikes me they can do the job better'n Charles Stuart.' Ratsford had adopted a pompous tone the better to enunciate the name by which the King had been referred to in his trial. 'All fer the best, if yer asks me,' he said, patting his knee and beckoning to her to please him by sitting on it.

'I've your dinner to see too,' she had temporised, handing him a full bumper of ale to keep him occupied.

On the day of the execution Ratsford had joined several of his friends and, like the rest of their neighbouring menfolk and a good deal of their wives, sallied to Whitehall. When he came back that evening he was roaring drunk and insisted Anne lay with him. Skilled at managing her objectionable husband, she fondled him until he spent himself and fell asleep. For months now her privities had been denied Ratsford; for months they had belonged to George Monck alone.

The thought recalled her to the letter that lay, momentarily neglected, in her lap. She took it up again, found she was unable to read it in the twilight and lit a candle. Ratsford had not come home and while she risked interruption, she felt compelled to finish it; she owed George that, and searched out the last passage again.

Then came the news of the King's trial and execution, which threw a petard among the hounds. The Scots would have none of any Republic, Ormonde declared the Prince of Wales King of the Three Kingdoms and sent emissaries to me and others, including O'Neill. Under the Papist Nuncio's influence O'Neill must have vacillated, but the rest of us gave our reply. Whether Ormonde supposed I would return to an earlier allegiance, I know not, but I knew of the great expedition meditated against Ireland and was bound in all honour, as commissioned, to serve the Parliament.

It had come to me in this uncertain period that some of my officers were becoming disaffected and, hearing the news of the King's execution and the declarations of Ormonde, I was suspicious of their loyalty. I pressed this matter upon them, seeking to bring it into the light, aware that by now some among them, mostly Scotchmen, objected to taking orders from the Regicides in London. Their eyes strayed towards Inchiquin and Ormonde, now in the country himself, whose superiority in cavalry I had sought to counter by a correspondence with Sir Thomas Fairfax, pleading an urgent reinforcement of a regiment of horse.

All I received was a secret instruction to ensure O'Neill with his eight-thousand men did not effect a junction with Ormonde and Inchiquin. This was pressed upon me as overriding all other considerations, for any such junction would prejudice the success of the forthcoming expedition.

Anne paused at the under-lining, unsure of its exact import but anxious at the emphasis and concluding the nature of the puzzle lay in the words 'secret instruction'. It occurred to her that – while she understood little of its detail or import – in this letter, Monck confided in her to a very great extent. She vaguely saw it as testamentary, but more shrewdly grasped his desire for her to keep it safe, along with his papers written in The Tower, an insurance against any enemy that later might seek to discredit him. This warmed her as she read on.

Next Ormonde moved on Dublin while Inchiquin advanced upon Trim. In the meanwhile O'Neill approached to within thirty miles of Dundalk where I then lay. I sent word to O'Neill, asking for a cessation between us, even an alliance, for three months and that he state his terms; they were mostly preposterous. Besides freedom of religion and the restoration of his lands in Tyrone, he demanded a senior post under Fairfax. It was nought but moonshine but I played him a game, gaining time.

Our cause was now in the gravest danger. Though O'Neill could be relied upon to remain quiescent for a short while, besides myself, only two other garrisons held out. With O'Neill and the Nuncio's confederation thrown in against us, Ormonde held the entire country and I was lost. Inchiquin, having taken Drogheda was at the gates of Dundalk. I sought O'Neill's assistance, for our terms included mutual assistance, but he pleaded a shortage of powder the supply of which formed the issue of which I stand now in dishonour.

But all was thrown away by treachery. My scheme was exposed, undermining my honesty, particularly in the eyes of my officers and I, unable to reveal the reasons why I had adopted the apparently inexplicable course of action that I did, am held to be a man of duplicity…

Anne crushed the letter in her lap. She understood this plainly enough. Her beloved George, his good name not only publicly impugned, but dishonoured among the very officers whose absolute loyalty he demanded and required, had suffered a terrible, terrible blow. Her eyes filled with tears as she continued to read.

I have subsequently found some support, but am unable to publicly justify my conduct and, for all the world to see, it must stand to my condemnation. There was a great necessity to act as I did, of that I am sure and I must accept that as my consolation: it was my duty, and nothing more nor less.

But all this having been revealed and O'Neill no longer to be relied upon, all but seventeen of my men – seventeen, please note – devoid of pay for many months, slipped over to Inchiquin and on a day I shall ever remember, July the 17th, your loving friend George Monck was obliged to surrender to the enemy. I negotiated terms advantageous to myself, though most of those officers who had shared my success in the harrowing of Ulster deserted to Inchiquin and Ormonde.

In ruling this country, it is necessary to do one of two things: either to root out and destroy the enemy and all those who support his faction without exception. Every priest and peasant, every woman, child and babe that has been baptised a Catholic must be put to the sword and not one seed from which the distemper can renew itself and again flourish must be suffered to remain, not even in the most distant extremities of the country. Or else one must continually embark in an endless negotiation, a ceaseless forestalling of intent, of outwitting the cunning resourcefulness of wilful children, children who see only the fizz of short-term victory, who care not for good governance but the conceit of advantage, howsoever temporary and illusory.

She was near the end now and thought she had heard the noise of her husband returning, but it was only the scuttering of a rat somewhere behind a wainscoting. The distraction made her pause for a moment and she re-read the last paragraph, frightened by Monck's uncompromising views, as images of women and children being put to the sword flashed before her mind's eye. Then she realised they were not dissimilar to odd sections of his long essay that, from time-to-time during their intimacy in The Tower, she had had her read out loud to him. The difference was that there they had merely been a written opinion but here, in his letter, it translated into a dreadful reality. With a shock she – who bore no personal animus against Catholics – perceived a terrible doctrine and glimpsed, for a moment, the burden of high command that he bore.

But Anne had never in her life read such a long letter, nor been aware of receiving such a great confidence. That George Monck was incapable of writing of anything other than his military profession never occurred to her. Why should it? She was struck instead with the paradox of loving this man whose kindness in taking notice of her delighted her; but from this rosy recollection arose another: she recalled the transformation of those kindly blue eyes into chips of ice; she recalled too the sense of power he was capable of emanating.

Great men must of necessity be of such a nature and George – *her* George – was indeed a great man. If she had ever doubted it, it was made plain by this letter which she now folded carefully, even reverentially. The strange mixture of tenderness and ruthlessness was what made great men differ from the likes of sots like Ratsford and his aimless cronies. But the dispassionate, indiscriminating murder of women and children ...? Anne Ratsford shuddered at the image of her George having hands steeped in the blood of the innocent.

She looked again at the folded sheets in her lap. From them she understood little of the events Monck described, but she regarded them as containing something akin to being sacred. Opening the sheets, she read the last sentence again before, at last, it occurred to her that it contained little of the personal and no signing off, affectionate or otherwise. There was no new page and it was not until she turned the last sheet over – the others having been covered only upon one side, as had been his practice when composing his essay in The Tower – that she found his last lines.

By the time you receive this, my fate will be decided and it mayhap that our pleasant trysts in The Tower shall resume. Whatever you hear of me, be assured my honour is intact. Please keep this letter safe and secure, dearest Anne, and place it with those other papers of mine which you hold. As for myself alone,

I am your ever faithful,

Geo. Monck

She looked again at the letter, tears filling her eyes as she shuffled the sheets. He called her 'dearest' and referred to himself as 'her loving friend' and 'ever faithful'. She knew well enough that he must remain circumspect and had promised nothing on his departure beyond his commitment to her. It had seemed enough then but now, knowing him to be in trouble, she wanted more, much more. From the vigour of Monck's handwriting, to say nothing of that underscoring, Anne could divine the fury and frustration of its author, even if she failed utterly to perceive that it was full of the prejudice of a Protestant Englishman at the wayward indifference of the

Irish and their refusal to accept the beneficent good-order of imposed – but foreign – government.

Instead, it occurred to her that such had been her haste that she had noted neither its place of origin, nor its date. She again shuffled the sheets and found upon the first two superscriptions that made her heart leap in her breast. It was Wednesday the 10th August: the letter bore a date of *August 4th* and its place of origin simply *Milford.* She had no idea where Milford was. Then she saw a scribbled line the ink of which had been smudged and suggested a last-minute addition: *I shall be in London within three or four days*.

'He is here!' she exclaimed, leaping to her feet, hearing a noise. This was no rat but a man's footfall. Her heart thundered in her breast as the door flew open. But, at that very moment, as Ratsford found his wife dewy-eyed over the correspondence of a stranger, George Monck stood before the Bar of a candlelit House of Commons awaiting his fate.

*

Six days earlier a travel-stained Monck had arrived on the shores of Milford Haven. The vast expanse of its landlocked harbour seemed full of ships, its surrounding fields and open country full of soldiers, tents, horse-lines and artillery parks. Monck noted the red-coats, the buff skirts and the quality of the equipment. He noted too, the boats in the harbour, crawling like water-beetles between shore and ships as the armament destined for Ireland embarked upon its crusade. Monck noted too that he was recognised, that men averted their faces and even swore, in that God-fearing way of the Puritan extremists, at his treachery. He had become inured to it, for it he had already encountered it at Chester, where he had landed from Ireland under the terms he had negotiated with Inchiquin after his one remaining drummer had beat a parley on the walls of Dundalk. Confronted with a surprising number of men in black, he had studiously avoided making any statement, even in the face of direct and unambiguous accusations of 'High Treason', owning only that his allegiance was to the Council of State and a declaration that he had acted – as he always acted in the public service – out of military necessity. But he was left in no doubt of his position in all this. Secret instructions or not, he, and he alone, was the scapegoat, the man who had betrayed the purity of the Protestant cause by treating with a Catholic chieftain. All he learned at Chester was that Oliver Cromwell was newly appointed Lord Lieutenant of Ireland and that he was then at Milford Haven. Monck had bought two horses and set out for Pembrokeshire.

He arrived on 4 August and made his way directly to Cromwell's headquarters at a small inn. Recognised by the staff officers, he was not kept waiting for long and soon found himself ushered into Cromwell's presence.

Cromwell sat at a table covered in papers; he did not look up, but continued writing. A clerk was gathering up his pens and ink-well; as he withdrew he threw Monck a glance that was as pitiful as it was curious. Cromwell continued working for some moments after the clerk had gone before laying down his pen and looking up at the travel-stained officer standing before him.

'General Monck,' he said rising and, leaning across the table, held out his hand. 'These are difficult times; please be seated.' He indicated that Monck should draw a plain upright chair that stood by the window towards the table. When both men had taken their seats Cromwell said, 'You have done well, though few will now, or ever, appreciate it …'

Monck said nothing, though he watched Cromwell closely.

Cromwell cleared his throat. 'There are, of course, those that hold you supped with the Devil, that you have compromised our expedition and dishonoured the innocent blood of the massacred. That much may be true, but as the God of Battles knoweth, there is also the matter of military necessity. Would you not agree?'

'Aye; but there is also the matter of your secret instructions,' Monck responded bluntly.

'Which were driven by military necessity, General, as I am sure you understand.' Unflinching, Monck met Cromwell's gaze, compelling him to further comment. 'Come, sir … you comprehend my meaning, do you not?'

'I am dishonoured and made a scapegoat, sir. My comprehension is of little importance since my future is uncertain and my good-name traduced.'

'You are going to have to trust me, General.'

'You are going into Ireland, sir. You will find business enough there to forget any obligation you might consider towards myself.'

'I may be a better judge of that than you, General. You must, of course, repair directly to London but whilst I am in no doubt that certain difficulties lie in wait for you there, I am confident that whatever they are, they will not result in charges the like of which you have faced before.'

Monck remained silent. He was boiling with suppressed anger, the fermentation not merely of his present woes, but of his serial disappointments, from Cadiz onwards. Nevertheless he knew the slightest manifestation of this weakness would destroy him in the good opinion of this influential man.

Cromwell met his scrutiny before asking in a mild tone of voice, 'You have come here directly from Ireland, have you not?'

Monck nodded. 'Aye, by way of Chester, where I was advised that you had been appointed Lord Lieutenant of Ireland and it was therefore proper to make my report to thee …' Monck paused a moment before adding, '… that and the fact that it was from your hand, by way of Captain Arthur, that I received your secret instructions.'

'We shall say no more of them, General,' Cromwell said firmly. 'You have thus far pleaded necessity; I further require you to take upon yourself the whole responsibility of your decision to treat with O'Neill …'

'I understand,' Monck broke in.

'You do?'

'The reasons of state are clear, sir,' Monck said simply. Cromwell looked shrewdly at Monck. While it would have been impertinent of Monck to have said more by way of explanation, it was clear to Cromwell, that he grasped all the import of the situation.

'Had you heard that Colonel Jones had engaged and prevailed over Ormonde at Rathminnes?'

'I had not, sir.'

'It is an astonishing mercy, so great and seasonable that it must stand to support us and strengthen our love and faith against more difficult times.'

'Indeed, sir, 'tis the best matter I have heard of, or has been said to me, these several weeks past.'

'I shall not forget you, General Monck, and before I embark I shall await the outcome of your summons to London, for thither thou must repair at once and with all despatch. Now, I beg you to retire for an hour to refresh yourself. Come again and I shall have letters to our friends in London. Should you wish to send word yourself, I have a courier leaving tomorrow. He shall carry a despatch of mine to the Council of State touching yourself. I would also have some discourse with you upon matters as they stood upon your leaving Ireland. That done you must make haste thither yourself.'

'Would your man carry a personal letter?'

'Of course,' Cromwell said rising. Monck rose with him and the General accompanied him to the door. Opening it he called for food, wine, wax, pen, paper and ink to be provided immediately for General Monck. An hour later the door opened again and Cromwell summoned him. Monck was just then sealing a long letter to Mistress Ratsford, a letter which he had begun some days earlier, the chief purpose of which was to calm himself and order his thoughts preparatory to being interviewed by those who would sit in judgement over him. It did not occur to him that Anne would make neither head nor tail of it.

Monck spent a further hour with the General learning that Coote had also treated with O'Neill but having thereby secured the city of Derry, would escape opprobrium. Cromwell also told him that Rinuccini was rumoured to have fled, remarking that Monck smiled at the news.

'You smile, General, why so?'

'He will be in despair at the squabbling of his partisans,' Monck said, adding, 'and there is in all this some advantageous consequence of my infamous conduct.'

'We must needs keep that to ourselves but tell me, in general principle, how …'

'Does one gain the upper hand?' Monck interrupted presumptuously, the final paragraphs of his letter to Anne coming readily to him. 'You must either destroy the enemy root-and-branch, sir, or sit down to endless negotiation and submit to an interminable succession of treacheries and betrayals while your forces are suborned, ambushed and whittled away. It is neither more nor less than that.'

Listening carefully, Cromwell nodded, asked a few peripheral questions after which he handed four letters to Monck, remarking that they were 'a shield of sorts'. He then asked if he had the private letter to which he had referred earlier which he required to be taken separately to London to add to his own despatch and Monck handed over his long missive to Anne. Without looking at the superscription, Cromwell called his clerk, handed the two papers over and held out his hand to Monck.

'Until we meet again,' he said and, turning to his clerk, added, 'See General Monck out, Thurloe.'

*

Monck rode hard for London, a solitary horseman with a spare mount trailing on a long rein. He fed and watered them regularly, changing horses at each stop and selling both at a loss at Bristol. His new horses, bought at an exorbitant and unhaggled price served him to Reading where he purchased a single gelding. He arrived in London and before resting, delivered Cromwell's four private letters, finally seeking sleep at an inn in Westminster. The following day he showed himself at Derby House and was ordered to reappear the next morning when the Council of State would hear what he had to say. It proved a difficult encounter and, though he had little time to recognise all its members he knew Lord Lisle, Earl Mulgrave, Sir Arthur Haselrig and Sir Thomas Fairfax. Although he detected friends among the members, some four of whom had been recipients of Cromwell's quartet of letters, the Lord President, John Bradshaw, ordered him to explain his actions in treating with O'Neill.

'It was a decision that was mine and mine alone,' Monck said, firmly, raking the assembled Council with his merciless eye. 'I plead nothing for myself but an understanding of military necessity. I was pressed on all sides and the temper of my men was being steadily worn-down by lack of pay …' The accusation was plain and he let it hang a moment to sting those members of the Irish Committee present with a condign reproach. 'A juncture between the Marquess of Ormonde and Owen Roe O'Neill would have proved immediately fatal to all our hopes but, with the preparations I knew to be in train respecting an imminent reinforcement, I had hopes that my motives would receive this Council's approval.'

'You had no instructions to act thus, General Monck?' he was asked by Lord Mulgrave.

'None, my Lord.'

'Not from any person of this Council not here present but whose authority you might have assumed carried the weight and opinion of us all?' Mulgrave gestured left and right. The allusion to Cromwell was clear and unambiguous and, again, Monck faced his interrogator.

'Not from any person, my Lord.'

'You were driven simply by the situation in which you found yourself?' asked Fairfax, not unkindly.

'Military necessity compelled me, with neither counsel nor instruction, to choose the lesser of two evils, Sir Thomas.'

Black Tom had been one of the recipients of Cromwell's letters and Honest George must needs dissemble. He had lied for Cromwell and yet his high-standing reputation for probity washed any suspicion from his interlocutors' minds. He watched as they sat back, looked from one to another and murmured amongst themselves. Monck noted that Lord Lisle avoided his eye and then Bradshaw ordered him to await a decision in an anteroom.

A quarter of an hour later he was summoned again and the Lord President addressed him.

'The Council has no powers to approve of your action, General,' Bradshaw said. 'Indeed the weight of opinion is against you and your action. Here, in this Chamber, we tend to disapprove of the entire matter, thinking it prejudicial to our great enterprise against the Irish rebels.' Bradshaw paused and Monck steeled himself: The Tower beckoned once again. And beyond The Tower perhaps something worse. Bradshaw cleared his throat and went on, 'You shall therefore make a report, and appear before the Bar of the House on Wednesday next. The Council will lay a formal request to this effect and it has been thus minuted. That is all.'

All hopes now dashed, Monck made his way back to his lodgings. The thought of Anne tempted him to walk to the City but any encounter with her in public would prove awkward and he had no wish to compromise her until he knew his fate. Besides, it would soon be known that he was in London and he had no wish to brave the ignorant prejudice of its opinionated citizens. Better that he kept his own company until he knew the outcome, though all he could realistically anticipate was a further incarceration in The Tower. That, he mused ruefully, would at least make it easy to contact Mistress Ratsford.

And perhaps, if he ever heard of it, Cromwell's intervention.

*

As bidden Monck appeared at the Bar of the House of Commons, eyeing the flutter of papers laid before the clerks and wondering which had a bearing upon his own case. It became rapidly clear that the news of the rout of Ormonde by Jones at Rathmines, resulting in the saving of Dublin, had only just arrived. Had Cromwell held Jones's express, and included it with his couriered despatch touching Monck himself? It seemed possible, even likely. But any comfort derived from this distant manipulation was dissolved as he was questioned, for the mood of the House was plainly hostile. There was, he was informed, evidence in his own hand, admitting to having some advice pertaining to the negotiations with O'Neill. Mystified as to the origin of this information, or the precise details, Monck was about to ask to see the relevant paper, when the Speaker, William Lenthall, asked him to name these advisers.

'I had no such advisers, sir. I did it upon my own score,' he replied staunchly, 'without the advice of any other persons. Only formerly I had some discourse of Colonel Jones, and he told me if I could keep off Owen Roe O'Neill and Ormonde from joining, it would be a good service.'

'Had you,' the Speaker continued, 'any advice or direction from Parliament, or the Council, or the Lord Lieutenant of Ireland, or any person here, to do it?'

Monck's response was deliberately categorical. 'Neither from Parliament, nor the Council, nor the Lord Lieutenant, nor any person here had I any advice or direction. Isolated as I was, I did it upon my own score for the preservation of the English interest there …' he paused, nodding at the papers lying on the table behind the mace, then added, '… and it has had some fruits accordingly.'

A murmur rose and the Speaker called for silence. Addressing Monck he said coldly, 'You shall withdraw, sir, and await our pleasure.' As Monck left the Chamber amid a rising crescendo of babble, he heard Speaker Lenthall call again for silence. Outside he settled to await his verdict. He could hear nothing but the swell of debate, which seemed interminable and afforded him at least the comfort of knowing opinion was divided. Occasionally a member emerged, threw a non-committal glance in his direction, before hurrying off on some business of his own. The day drew on and members whom he recognised as having left earlier, came back again to glance pityingly at his lonely figure as they re-entered the Chamber.

Eventually he heard the rise of general comment and the Speaker's voice ring clear above the racket. Someone came out and told him that the House was about to divide on the question of whether it approved the proceedings of General Monck. Again the noise increased and then, sometime later, it subsided again and his informant returned to state that it did not. Again a rising noise and a second motion was proposed; he learned that the members were about to divide on a vastly more ponderous issue. His informant pressed a piece of paper in his hand on which a hasty contraction of the motion had been scribbled.

That the H, do utterly disapprove – the innocent blood that has been shed is so fresh in this H.'s memory – that this H. do' detest and abhor the thoughts of any closing with any Popish rebels who h've had their hand in shedding blood. Amendm't added – that Col. M's conduct excusable on grounds of necessity.

Monck stared down at it, wondering who had laid down the amendment. Without it he would likely hang and he felt his heart thump as he recognised the imminent danger he was in. Somehow it was worse than that frozen instant in the breach at Breda when, it had seemed to him, he had stood quite alone in plain sight of the multitude of the enemy. But that moment of exposure had passed, to reserve him for another fate. Better he had been blown into eternity as an honest soldier, leader of a forlorn hope whose death could at least atone for his sins and lay glory to his name. Now …

Within the Chamber the noise gave nothing away as the debate proceeded and the time passed. Candles were next called for and, as the doors to the Chamber opened to admit them, Monck heard someone shout for vengeance against the massacred. After his weary months of campaigning in Ireland, it astonished Monck to hear this emotional rallying call. It was true that many innocent Protestants had been martyred for their stubborn faith, but so too had many Catholics, as his own ruthless harrying of the helpless peasants bore eloquent witness. It was madness to assume ends could be reached without violence; but the trick was to temper that violence, to apply only that much as was necessary to achieve the objective, and afterwards deal fairly with the enemy. 'Harm no man beyond what war demands,' Monck muttered to himself, forgetful of his root-and-branch advice to Cromwell and feeling a growing contempt for these extreme vapourings, uttered by men as distant from immediate danger as was the moon from the earth. What, in God's name, could he expect from these people?

'These are difficult times,' he recalled Cromwell saying. And: 'I shall not forget you …'

Placed where he now was, such assurances, no doubt kindly meant, signified nothing. And then he recalled Cromwell's assurance that he would await news of the outcome of Monck's summons before sailing for Ireland. At the time of its utterance it had seemed but one more reassuring kindness. Now, it was ominous. If Monck had not lied on Cromwell's behalf, the Lord Lieutenant stood to be recalled, destroying all hope of whatever Cromwell and his party of friends stood for and intended to do in this new Republic.

Sunk in this reverie Monck was lost for a while to the events on the far side of the Chamber doors. Suddenly, however, they flew open and a throng of people tumbled out to grasp his hand, to slap his back and to shout at him that they knew all along that Honest George was a man of unimpeachable probity.

'Some of them wanted you committed to The Tower, General!' a well-wisher shouted from the back of the red-faced crowd.

'Better The Tower was committed to you, sir,' bellowed another, as a wave of guffaws met this witticism.

'General Monck. A word, sir, if you please. Gentlemen, pray make way.' It was Black Rod, confirming the news the pack of friendly members had borne from the Chamber of the House. 'The motion was carried in your favour to the extent of remonstrating with the evil of the matter but that your conduct was excusable,' James Maxwell pronounced solemnly. 'You are free to go, General.'

Monck, suddenly unable to speak, made his bow and was borne out into the soft August darkness by the throng. But he thought no longer of himself, only of Anne.

*

By the end of the week Monck woke to the news that an account exonerating him had been published 'by Authority'. An opposition hack calling himself 'The Man in the Moon' entitled this public exculpation 'a blindation', an opinion with which Monck privately agreed, but people forgot all the popularly cited 'evidence' heaped against him, chiefly his previous stubborn loyalty to the King and with it the taint of 'malignancy'. Where previously he had hardened himself against hostile glares, he now found himself cheered, such was the fickle nature of public opinion. Lord Lisle sought him out and told him – was there something meaningful in Lisle's sober tone? – that on 12 August 'Oliver had sailed'.

Monck met the news with the rejoinder that he was happy the great expedition was at last under way, adding that, 'The pity of it was that he himself was unemployed.'

'Then you must complete writing your military theories, General,' Lisle said encouragingly. 'I should much like to see them.'

Monck bit off an admission they had been finished long ago and nodded. It was only afterwards that he chid himself; he was becoming too accomplished a liar and must guard against it in the future.

He finally quit the Westminster inn and took up lodgings in the City, sending a boy with a note to Anne, along with instructions to await a reply. He never saw the boy again; instead Anne came that evening to his rooms bearing a bag containing some personal effects and his papers. She had a black-eye, the side of her head seemed strangely contused and her eyes were red and swollen with crying. So badly was she disfigured that, for a moment Monck failed to recognise her.

'Anne?' Then: 'For the love of God come in, come in! Tell me who did this to you.' He took the bag from her and drew her inside his rooms. 'Was this Ratsford? The damned scoundrel!'

'He has gone,' she said, falling sobbing, into his arms. 'Oh, George, George, how I have longed for you …'

'Come, you are safe now,' he said soothingly, vowing to settle matters with Ratsford on the morrow.

He was astir early next morning. For all her battered state, he was immensely cheered by the appearance of Anne in his bed. He looked across at her, still sleeping, then attended to some letters newly arrived, but which had been following him round for some few weeks. The discharge of Parliament, though it deprived him of any hope of a command, lightened his spirits so much that it was only after the burden had been lifted that he realised the extent of the yoke he had borne in Ireland. Anne would heal, he thought looking at her, and Oliver had promised …

For a moment it struck him that he would not now be happy to get a summons from Cromwell to join him in Ireland; he had had a bellyful of Ireland. With Anne estranged from the loathsome Ratsford and no immediate employment in prospect for himself, he must consider what should be done.

He impatiently slit the seal of one of the letters, fearful that it might be a summons to attend the Lord Lieutenant in Dublin but it brought news of a sadder kind. His older brother Tom had been killed by a fall from his horse and George was notified that he was heir-in-tail to Potheridge. He looked again at the letter and found it had been written over eighteen months earlier, lost to him as he campaigned in Ireland. The lateness of this sad intelligence seemed to add to the burden of imposition a mere execution of his duty had laid upon him and, for a moment he teetered on the brink of giving way to the red rage that, after all his tribulations seemed about to engulf him. But, at that moment, Anne stirred and woke with a groan at the pain in her face. Their eyes met and, sensing something wrong, she asked, 'What is it?'

'My brother Thomas is dead. Do you remember I told you something of my family in the West Country?'

'Aye, I do, and I know you for a Devon man,' she said smiling awkwardly, having long liked his burr.

'This letter has taken over a year to reach me …'

'You did not write to me for even longer.'

'Did I not?' he asked sharply, looking at her directly.

'No George, you did not.'

He lowered his eyes again at the letter in his lap. 'Then I am sorry for it, my dear, truly sorry …' Monck sighed and smote his thigh. 'Brother Tom, brother Tom,' he said in a voice full of regret, then felt the warmth of Anne's body close to him, and her arms about his shoulder. He looked up at her bruised face and smiled. 'I think we must go down into Devon,' he said, 'for there are matters of business to which I have to attend and to which my attention is long overdue.'

'*Our* attention, George,' she whispered in his ear.

'Aye,' he agreed indulgently and turning he kissed her again. 'Aye, Anne, *our* attention.'

POTHERIDGE

Summer 1649 – June 1650

They had left London for the West Country after a brief but fruitless attempt to find Ratsford. No-one knew of his whereabouts, not even his drinking cronies. Someone thought Ratsford might have taken ship, though with what prospects it was unclear. As Anne herself remarked, there were few opportunities for a mixer of perfumed waters aboard any vessel but Monck, recalling his service aboard the *Perseus*, could divine the train of thought that might have led the errant Ratsford towards the forest of masts and spars that crowded London's pool. It appeared, however, that prior to whatever departure he had contrived, Ratsford had enjoyed an evening of free-spending. Moreover he had, as Anne discovered with a shock, stolen the cache of money she had put by, hidden in a secret place behind the rough panelling of their rooms.

'I did not know he knew of it,' she said furiously at the revelation of her husband's infamy.

'Drunkards are uncommon cunning,' Monck soothed, adding, 'Do not fret, I have just sufficient for the two of us …'

For Anne, her husband's theft was a double outrage, for she had been hoarding the money against the day when she would be free of her brutal spouse and able to establish herself independently. 'But this was *mine*, George, *mine*,' she bewailed, 'money I had earned myself and to which he had no right! It is plain theft, damn him!'

This was a side of her he had never previously seen and he found it pleasing. 'Your spirit does you credit Anne, but his actions give you grounds for leaving him …'

She blew out her cheeks and paused, looking at him and seeing the import of his words in his blue eyes. 'Grounds for leaving him …' she repeated, uncertainly.

'Aye …'

'He has certainly left me,' she said, mindful of the lost purse. 'And taken twenty-two sovereigns … Everything …'

'*All* your savings? And in gold,' Monck remarked. It lent colour to those hints of both carefulness and cupidity that he had suspected in her. She would not be a woman to squander a man's substance, he thought, not that brother Tom's inheritance had left him over much beyond a trail of entailments, annuities and debt.

'What use is base coin?' Anne was saying dismissively, adding that: 'It is lucky he did not have the gold the King sent you.'

'Well, he did not, so there is an end to the matter. Now come away, I have horses and a carriage awaiting us. You will find Potheridge more congenial than the stews of London. Let us put an end to all this.'

He had proved right. Anne, who had never ventured beyond the City bounds, had shown a childish delight throughout the journey, seemingly unaware of its discomforts, its flea-ridden inn beds in which they tumbled among the filthy sheets, the rain rutted roads, or the abominable jolting of the conveyance. Despite struggling against a hard wind and sleet which met them on Salisbury Plain they stopped briefly to wonder at the megaliths of Stonehenge. After four days they descended into the valley of the Torridge and Anne was utterly beguiled by the narrow sunken lanes and the prospect of the old house as it emerged from the trees and Monck told her they were almost at the end of their journey.

After leaning out of the carriage window to peer ahead she drew back into its gloomy interior and regarded him, her eyes aglow, her voice tremulous with wonder. 'Why George, George,' she asked breathlessly, as if scarce able to comprehend her changed circumstances, 'is this now all yours?'

It was indeed, but it came with problems of its own and for Monck the weeks that followed were a mixture of pain and pleasure. He recaptured something of his lost youth in the company of his younger brother Nicholas, who was the incumbent in the distant parish of Plymtree, a hard day's ride across the county, and fell into the easy habit of riding over once a month or so. Nicholas had none of George's fire-in-the-belly, but was bookish and gently-mannered, as behove a man of the cloth. A staunch Royalist, Nicholas disapproved of brother George serving Parliament, but Monck persuaded him, as he had persuaded Wren, that he was both pragmatist and patriot and wrought in the first place for the good of the country.

'You have the cure of souls, brother,' he concluded, fixing Nicholas with his blue eyes so that his brother, like Wren before him, perceived something of the man Monck could be upon the battlefield. 'But I have a duty towards them while they live and seek to provide for their families. Parliament has at least established a kind of peace over England and that most are grateful for.'

'Perhaps …' Nicholas had conceded, unwilling to fall-out with his elder sibling. However, as man of the cloth, Nicholas was less forgiving of his wayward brother when it came to the matter of Anne Ratsford. He made his views known, pointing out to George the impropriety of him attending church in the company of his mistress and refusing to receive her in his rectory.

Monck had shrugged. 'So be it; that is your privilege, but I have it in mind to engage her by a handfasting,' he said firmly.

'Then she is free to marry?' Nicholas asked sharply. 'Remember adultery is not only a mortal sin, but a capital offence and rumour has it that she is another man's wife.'

'Rumour has laid other charges against me, Nick.' Monck evaded the direct question. 'Tell me, do they still say hereabouts that I was the cause of Battyn's death?'

'Battyn?'

'Aye, Battyn. He that was under-sheriff of Devon.'

Nicholas frowned and shook his head. 'I have not heard it said for many a long year.' The younger man adopted a thoughtful expression, as though reviewing a catalogue of gossip, leaving Monck to conclude that he had diverted Nicholas from the point of his question about Anne. He rose with a sigh.

'I cannot stay longer. There is rain coming, I have a hard ride and there is much to be done at the manor.'

'Aye, Tom was no better than father when it came to the estate.' Nicholas rose and scratched his head, his eyes suddenly brightening. 'I tell you what,' he said, 'let me introduce you to Will Morrice. He is a shrewd fellow and might well serve you by way of advice, for he administers our old Uncle Bevil's affairs now he is in Abraham's bosom.'

Monck nodded his acquiescence and returned resignedly to the wretched business of putting the estate upon a better footing. Whether or not Morrice would prove of any help he did not know, though he had agreed to an overture being pursued by Nicholas if only to prevent him returning to moralising. But to his surprise Monck had found that his eye for detail, a military skill engendered by old Henry Hexham, revealed several areas by the means of which he could improve things and so he settled to the matter, spending hours every day either at his ledgers or walking his land and speaking with his tenants. The small amount of money he had by way of back-pay allowed him to make some modest, improving investments and he held out high hopes for the following year.

While Anne felt something of neglect from all this, she was quick to understand that despite the rolling hills, the silver river which wound its way through the dense woodland, Potheridge was on the edge of ruin. She was also shrewd enough to know that George, in both their interests, must be allowed to rectify this, a matter in which her meddling – beyond a little encouragement from time to time – would not be appreciated. Instead she familiarised herself with the household and relieved Tom's widow, a woman who wore her weeds heavily, of the burden of this task.

Intelligent and practical, Anne had soon overcome most of the servants' mistrust of their new Cockney mistress and, despite the fact that she and the Master were unmarried, had won a large measure of their respect largely by her ability to roll up her sleeves and apply herself to the meanest of the daily tasks. Publicly the household was a scandal, but ever since Old Sir Thomas had plunged the family and the estate into extremity, Potheridge had acquired an air of irredeemable decline.

None of these considerations troubled Monck and Anne as the weeks passed into months and the anniversary of their arrival seemed not so far off. They settled easily to the way of life and Monck, devoted to his task on his farms, began to forget his military ambitions. Despite his robust attitude towards his brother he was troubled by his relationship with Anne, a factor that he would have to resolve if they were to settle at Potheridge and take up the life of a country squire and his lady. His visits to Nicholas failed to wear-down his brother's refusal to meet Anne, or to persuade him and his wife to at least accept an invitation to stay at the manor. Nicholas's inflexibility irritated Monck and he cursed Ratsford for not dying like a decent fellow. God knew there was enough cholera in London to kill off a dozen Ratsfords weekly and while he might die from scurvy or catch the Great Pox from the whores of Leghorn if he had indeed taken ship, the suspicion of his still being alive lay like a cloud over the lovers.

But, to their mutual delight, they loved well and, besides that, lived well off the game that the estate provided. In their idle moments, they wandered in the woods that so luxuriantly overhung the silver Torridge. Anne was transported by delight at this truly idyllic turn in her adventure with her beloved George, boosted as it was with all the beauteous novelty of the countryside to a city-bred woman. She could not contain her wonder when Monck bade her to silence and they crept up on a badger's sett outside which a family of the animals rolled in the twilight. On one golden evening Monck pointed out a pair of otters sporting in the shallows of the river and he tried to teach her, unsuccessfully as it happened, to tickle for trout. In turn she chuckled at the sight of Monck, his thick-set body lying prone on a little overhang of the greensward along the river's bank, one arm in the cold water. And she clapped her hands like a child when, with a sudden motion, his arm flew up and a gleaming fish flew through the air to land gasping at her feet.

On one particular evening in late May, as the setting sun showed through the trees and dappled the wavelets of the river with gold, the two of them were sauntering hand-in-hand along a short reach of the river of which they had become fond, when it occurred to Monck that he was perhaps being compensated for his strange, disturbed boyhood. And while they stood and watched as the otters appeared with two young, Anne's eye was caught by the sapphire blue flash of a small bird that disappeared in the reeds seemingly as soon as it had revealed itself.

'What was that?' she asked.

'A kingfisher,' Monck replied, smiling.

'A kingfisher. That seems somewhat like unto magic,' she said, wondering.

'Aye, perhaps it was.' Monck stopped and drew her close to him. 'I have neither ring nor keepsake upon me for you Anne, but if you wilt have me I am for thy handfasting.'

Her eyes filled at this formal announcement of intent, binding between lovers even in law. Words failed her, though she tried to speak. She wanted nothing more and, after a few moments during which they kissed and embraced, she said as much.

'I would have spoken to my brother long since …' he began, his voice tailing off, 'but for …'

'But for the matter of my husband.'

'But for the matter of thy husband, yes. I have not told you, but my brother has some notion … had heard some tittle-tattle that you are not free to marry …'

'Think you that I did not know,' she responded with a hint of indignation. 'Why else would he shun me and refuse to wait upon you at the manor, for all the thirty odd miles that lie between us and him?'

'I am sorry …'

''Tis not your fault, George but …'

'But what?'

'He will not come back to me, and if he should we may buy him off.'

Monck shook his head. ''T would be a precarious foundation for a marriage.'

She drew away from him and gestured round them. 'Not if we are buried away amid these trees,' she exclaimed, unwilling for the shadow of Ratsford to spoil the occasion of Monck's proposal.

'Is that what we shall be, buried away amid the trees?' He smiled sadly.

'What else?' she said simply and he shrugged. It was not only Ratsford who threw shadows. The sun was all but down now and the chilly damps of twilight were not far off. Yesterday at brother Nicholas's he had learned that Cromwell was back from Ireland and that Sir Thomas Fairfax had been appointed commander-in-chief of a new expedition intended for Scotland.

'There are rumours that Fairfax has turned the appointment down,' Nicholas informed Monck.

'Rumours, eh? Well, well, and why are we keen to chastise the Scots? Are we so set to take up cudgels against the Covenant?' All Monck's ire against oaths was compressed into a question that was, essentially, rhetorical.

'Perhaps,' said Nicholas, 'but 'tis said that the Scottish Covenanters have agreed that if he agrees to sign the Covenant himself and to establish Presbyterianism in England and Ireland, Charles Stuart may return from exile and shall be crowned King of Scotland.'

Now Monck, standing under the trees hand-in-hand with Anne perceived a happiness within his reach, a prospect which for an hour or so had driven all thoughts of Nicholas's news from his mind, gave a sudden shudder at the implications of the intelligence.

'You are cold?' Anne asked rubbing his back as they turned and began to walk back to the house.

'No, but grey geese are flying over my grave.'

'That is not an expression I much like,' Anne said.

'No. I'm sorry.' But the shadow of premonition had spoiled the handfasting for Monck, just as had that of Ratsford for Anne.

*

They did not mention their handfasting during the following week, bound by a mutual, if unspoken, agreement to suppress the matter. This had Anne privately weeping and Monck walking his land in an uncommonly foul mood and they ate in a near silence that had the servants gossiping. It was concluded that the Master had tired of his doxy and, while they would be sorry to see her go for she was a pleasant enough creature when the Master smiled upon her, they would not be surprised. Monck failed to visit his brother at the beginning of June, but they bumped into each other as Nicholas, thinking George to be ill and having heard something of trouble at Potheridge threw off his prejudice, exercised a Christian forbearance and made his way towards the old house in which he had spent his childhood, unlike its present resident.

Both were embarrassed when the fortuitous encounter took place. Nicholas sought to explain his whereabouts but failed and neither man knew what to say for a moment. Then Monck sighed and offered his hand up to Nicholas on his nag.

'Damnation, Nick, I have need of thy company and thy advice. Come, walk with me.' As the two men fell in step Monck admitted a degree of discord but wondered how it had reached Plymtree until Nicholas revealed he had received a letter from their joint sister-in-law. Suddenly confidential, Monck outlined the problem of Ratsford and the situation as regarded Anne before falling expectantly silent.

'So you have plighted your troth?'

'There was a handfasting of sorts,' Monck explained awkwardly.

'But you have no evidence of the husband's death?'

Monck shook his head. 'No. Only of his desertion and that is mere circumspection.'

'So any form of marriage, even a clandestine ceremony in the Fleet or at the Mint would be bigamous.'

'So it would seem.'

Nicholas stopped, facing his brother who was compelled to stop and stare at him. 'Then there is nothing I can do for you.'

Monck stared at his brother, then looked away. 'No.' He sighed. 'Well then, we shall have to continue our life of sin,' he said shortly. 'Will you come to the house and meet the lady?'

'I think it better that I should not.'

'Huh. Very well. Then good day to you brother Nicholas,'

Nicholas Monck watched as the sturdy figure strode off. He shook his head. 'No good will come of this,' he said to himself, before turning his horse, remounting and heading back on the long ride to Plymtree.

*

Monck returned to the manor much changed and his mood rapidly transformed that of Anne. The rejection of Nicholas had ignited his old rage and, in an attempt to control it he walked with a brisk fury. Such was the swiftness of his mental processes that he was of a sudden taken by an idea. He did not tell her of it, only that he would shortly leave for London, alone, and with the intention of fully resolving the matter of Ratsford. That night they made love and the following morning the servants remarked that the Master and his mistress had broken their fast in the jolliest of circumstances. But the elation that was felt throughout Potheridge manor at the resumption of daily life untrammelled by unhappiness was short-lived, for the day brought two horsemen to the front door. The pot-helmeted cavalry cornet with a red sash jumped from his mount with a peremptory air of expectation, handing his horse's reins to the jack-booted trooper that accompanied him. Having gained attention at the door the cornet thumped into the house asking for General Monck.

Anne appeared and offered refreshment while word was sent for the Master who was in the woods hunting a fallow buck for the pot. When he arrived home the two men retired for half an hour, after which the cornet remounted his horse and he and his companion clattered away.

'What is it, George?' Anne asked anxiously, guessing it was summons the men had brought.

'Oliver is repaying a debt …'

'What mean you? He does not owe you money, does he?'

Monck laughed. 'No. Something of greater value. It does not matter. I am requested to join the Army and am appointed a Supernumerary Colonel and Acting Lieutenant General of the Artillery.'

Anne had no idea what any of this meant except that, from the look of him, there was no question that Monck was about to leave her. He saw what was in her mind, stepped forward slipping his arm about her waist and before she had a chance to remonstrate said: 'This will settle all matters, both between ourselves, for we shall be married upon my return, and between myself and Parliament …'

'*Parliament*?' she queried with a frown.

'They reprimanded me, Anne, let me go upon an excuse. Oliver knows the truth and is reinstating me.'

She did not – could not – understand the import of what he was confiding but he was again, suddenly, the great man she had been in awe of when she had washed and ironed his shirts in The Tower. She knew she had neither the power nor the right to stand in his way, though her heart sank within her.

'What of me?' she whispered.

'You will stay here. You will be safe and you may continue to run the house, God knows someone must. I shall send word for Nicholas and you shall meet him before I go. Come, all will be well and for the best …'

'What of my husband?' she hissed, fearful of someone overhearing them, for the house seethed with the news of the cavalrymen's visit and seemed already disturbed at the prospect of changing circumstances.

'I shall deal with the matter, as I promised, and we *shall* be married. It is already June, Anne. I shall be back in London by the winter. Ratsford will be disposed of and you and I shall marry.'

She was confused, at once happy and terrified, on the verge of tears and forced to smile. Men did not always return from war and even Lieutenant Generals of whatever it was were no proof against sword thrust or shot any more than the beautiful fallow buck that hung bleeding in the yard.

In the two days that followed she watched him, as though from a great and increasing distance, make his preparations for departure, ordering the affairs of the estate, entertaining Nicholas and his wife at an awkward but not entirely unsuccessful dinner, gathering his kit and selecting his three horses. She felt the steady encroachment of separation, its icy fingers prising them apart as she privately realised something else, something that uncertainty prevented her from informing him of, though she wished to: that she might have conceived.

And then he was gone.

DUNBAR

September 1650

'Steady men, steady!'

Monck's voice seemed lost in the drizzle and the close blackness of the wet night. He looked left, along the line of his own pike-men whose shapes were soon indistinct in the sodden gloom, betrayed only by the pallid gleam of helmets and pike-heads. To his right Reade's men stood in echelon, right flank refused. Far to the left and out of sight lay Hacker's foot.

'Colonel Hacker!' he shouted. 'Do your men stand, sir?'

'As a rock, General Monck!' Hacker's reassuring voice called back out of the night.

Monck's position lay across the main road to Berwick, along which General David Leslie's Scots had harried them all day. Somewhere behind Monck's rear-guard the horse and foot of General Cromwell's New Model Army sought bivouacs and the balm of sleep amid a cluster of bothies and stone walls that formed a small deserted habitation on the road west of Haddington. The lucky few among them were wracked by no more than the pangs of hunger and the lassitude of fatigue, but most suffered the humiliating and unpredictable promptings of dysentery, the shivers of fever and ague, and all were soaked to their skins after days of retreat.

Only Monck's iron will and ruthless discipline had held the rear-guard to its task, as now it had faced about and awaited Leslie's cavalry. Leslie knew his enemy; he had fought alongside Cromwell and Fairfax at Marston Moor and had the measure of his opponents. And Monck had met him before, as he had told King Charles in Christchurch garden. Always circumspect in the presence of the foe, Monck marked the encounter with particular care. Disintegration of the rear-guard, easy enough on such a wet night amid the extremity of privation, would be disastrous. The English Army in Scotland would be destroyed and if that happened – as seemed likely in the extremity of its circumstances – God alone knew what would be the consequences for England. That his rear-guard stood in the face of that awesome cataclysm was the conceit that held Monck to his charge that foul night.

His pickets had come in half-an-hour earlier with tales of the jingle of harness and Monck's intuition told him Leslie would make one more attack that day – or perhaps it was the first of the next, for it must be close to midnight. Monck hefted his officer's half-pike; undeterred by the appalling conditions or the weight of his great responsibility. It gave him a grim satisfaction, for to serve 'from the pike up' was the only path by which a soldier of fortune – as he had once been – could begin to mount the ladder of military achievement and this melding of command of the rear-guard with the dire necessity of having to stand as a common pike-man to put heart into his demoralised men was much to Monck's liking.

He knew that few among the distinguished but essentially amateur warriors that held high commands of the English Army in Scotland were inclined to undertake – or incapable of achieving – that duty of holding men together under such duress. This included not only Fleetwood and Lambert, but the Captain General, Oliver Cromwell himself, who was nervously biting his nails to the very quick for fear of the trap he had led his army into. Had God deserted them?

Monck chuckled grimly to himself; not if he had anything to do with it! Besides this grave charge was Oliver's reward for his own secret service to the Captain-General. Now, thought Monck, there was an irony!

Behind him his men grew restless; murmuring ran hither and yon through the ranks and in a low growl he called for silence. The men obeyed at once, word being passed down the line. Monck sensed movement out there in the darkness and even as he stood in the sodden morass of roadside grass he felt through the wet soles of his boots the ground tremble under the steady advance of Leslie's cavalry.

'Pass the word,' he growled again to left and right, his voice level and striving not to alarm the oncoming horse, 'to stand to, present pikes, musketeers to make ready!'

'Aye, sir, stand-to, present pikes and make ready!'

He heard the company sergeants pick it up and the urgent whisper vanished into the darkness on either flank. As the word passed down the line he saw the ripple of pike-heads as their hafts were dug in at the boot and the sharp points lowered, inclined ready to receive the oncoming cavalry: at least they might surprise Leslie a little. Monck hoped at least some of the musketeers had glowing slow-matches in their gunlocks.

After a few moments pregnant with suspense, out of the wet darkness all along the front, emerging like ghosts, came the nodding heads of horses and the faint gleam of rain on helm, cuirass and sword-blade.

'Give fire!'

The volley was sporadic, a spluttering coughing, the powder of many damp and ineffectual, but the enemy's horses baulked at the sudden appearance out of the rain of the steady, steel-tipped ranks of Monck's infantry. Horses did not like pikes and their riders did not enjoy the flailing of leaden balls the musketeers – posted in the intervals between the companies of pike-men – now flung among them. It had been a long day and the rain dampened the ardour of the weary attackers and while the musket balls rattled rather than killed, others galled the jittery horses. A few gallant souls came on until their mounts, eyes gleaming, their hard-bitten mouths foaming at the constraint of their bits, turned aside. Fewer still, pressed by those behind them, near impaled themselves on the steel hedge, whereupon Monck seized his opportunity.

'Advance pikes!' he roared, and the front ranks thrust forward two or three steps; it was enough. Horses reared and screeched with pain as some pike-men found a target. Somewhere to Monck's left a cavalry man lost his seat and fell with a mixture of clattering armour and the dull, sodden thud of bodily impact, to be trampled under the enraged and frightened hooves of his own horse.

'Back! Back!' Monck heard someone in authority cry, and a trumpet brayed the order to retire. Monck went forward, over the few dead and wounded – horses and men pressed into the mire. God! What a country for campaigning! He was followed by his company captains who, with drawn swords, despatched the wounded, both troopers and their mounts. It was a grimly bloody but necessary business and his subordinates were harshly professional. Confident that he had seen the last of the Scots for the night, Monck halted his men and returned to the line, ordering the men to lay down on their arms and the captains to post their pickets again. Finding a spot under the lee of a dry-stone wall Monck sat down, pulled his wide-brimmed hat down over his eyes, wrapped his cloak tightly around him and went to sleep. The last thought that went through his mind before the sleep of exhaustion overcame him was that there would be more such work to do on the morrow. And that it would be raining.

The following day it was clear that although Monck had thrown back Leslie's half-hearted probe on the rear of the retreating English, the Scottish general had out-marched them on the right. Much of Leslie's force was now ahead of them, occupying the hummock of Doon Hill, a commanding spur of the Lammermuir Hills that lay just south of the road to Berwick. During a day of constant drizzle falling from an overcast sky, wherein a low mist obscured a full view of the Scots movements, detachments of Leslie's Covenanters came down from the hill and extended their line northwards, towards the coast and the town of Dunbar, barring the Berwick road to the south-east. Their line of retreat now blocked, the English Army was cut off.

'We must now needs stand and fight,' Monck growled to Major Abraham Holmes.

'And needs must die to save Oliver's neck,' Holmes responded.

'Happen that will be the fate of some among us,' Monck agreed.

''Tis a pity it has come to this.'

'Aye.' Monck looked at his subordinate and grinned: 'But that is always a possibility for a soldier.'

Holmes stared at him for a moment and then caught his meaning and smiled back with a chuckle. ''Tis in God's hands …'

'God may need a little help,' said Monck mounting the horse that had been led up on his orders.

All day Monck, attending to the duty that was rightfully Lambert's, brought forward the English units and deployed them along the line of the Broxburn as it roared in spate from the hills to the sea through small but precipitate ravines and wider, shallower crossing places.

For their part, the enemy closed the trap. As the day drew to a close the English Army was entrapped, and knew it. Psalm-singing seemed the only remedy most colonels of the New Model could devise for this circumstance; they were not used to finding themselves in so dreadful a position under such foul conditions. Nor were they used to contemplating ruinous defeat.

During the late afternoon, Monck had passed once through headquarters. A seated Cromwell had been pouring over a map, biting his lower lip, with Lambert standing beside him in – or at least so Monck thought – an attitude of piety designed to conjure up the help of Almighty God. He called his own small staff about him and set about posting pickets to cover the Army's rear and to secure his own especial responsibility, the artillery train.

'You see, gentlemen,' he said at one dismal point as the wind began to rise and blew their mud-caked cloaks about their wet legs, 'Leslie has no artillery to speak of; a few light guns, so all is not quite lost.'

Afterwards a few of his own officers, Holmes included, recalled that alone amongst the English, only General Monck exhibited any optimism that dreadful day. Tough and dutiful, he was still at his rounds long after dark, apparently oblivious of the hopelessness of the Army's situation. There were some, even among the beleaguered staff, who thought it clear evidence that George Monck was none too bright.

*

'Douse that lantern!'

Monck heard the muttered remark this order prompted and stopped, to turn on the three young officers trailing in his wake. The fitful lantern-light fell upon a shiny slurry of wet earth, mud-caked boots and the three dejected forms as they stood in their sodden cloaks lashed by wind and rain. The light was extinguished and the impenetrable gloom closed round them, isolating them as individuals even as they stood close together.

'You will see better when your eyes have grown accustomed to the darkness,' Monck said kindly, ignoring the hint of insubordination, for they were exhausted and his order to accompany him as he made his last rounds of the lines and the artillery park in the Army's rear, had sorely tested their obedience. They did not want a homily but they deserved one.

'It is precisely now, gentlemen, when we are caught in so parlous a position as we now find our Army, that we must most exert ourselves. Such,' he added, his tone hardening, 'is the *duty* of officers.' He stared unseeing in their direction for a moment, then turned and walked on, his boots slithering and squelching in the mud churned up by the horses and handful of carts that had been hauled out of harm's way a few hours earlier.

They were indeed in a parlous state. The English Army's back was to the sea where the only escape was in an inadequate handful of store-ships lying in Dunbar harbour. To their front – towards the south-east – now firmly deployed across the road to Berwick-on-Tweed and the English border, lay twenty-three thousand Scots Covenanters under the able command of David Leslie. The Scots Army was more than twice the size of the force under Oliver Cromwell which, after an eight day march in appalling weather through country stripped of supplies, had failed in Cromwell's objective of quickly seizing Edinburgh. In evading a decisive action, Leslie had exhausted the English Army, tempting Cromwell into a series of fruitless probing engagements, his guns of insufficient weight-of-metal to blast their way through Leslie's carefully constructed defences.

Unable to recruit all their necessities at Musselburgh, the invaders had been compelled to retreat, with Leslie and his moss-troopers in hot and eager pursuit. Reduced to a bare ration of stale cheese and biscuit, forced to drink burn-water or looted small beer, the English soldiers rapidly succumbed to the bloody flux as they tramped wearily through the sodden countryside under lowering skies, incessant rain and gales of wind.

Now, to add to their misery, they had been outmanoeuvred by the enemy. Tomorrow they would be forced to fight and, as he trudged wearily through the mud, surrounded by the howling darkness of the wet and windy night, Monck reflected upon the likely outcome. They lay in Leslie's palm and Cromwell's vaunted reputation looked likely to be overturned. The English Army in Scotland – the New Model Army – was no longer in good spirits, for all its psalm-singing self-belief in its God-given destiny. The retreat in relentless rain, the lack of provisions and outbreaks of dysentery had, with the constant harrying of the Scots, seriously undermined the English soldiers' morale. Their physical and moral condition was so compromised that even God, it seemed, had abandoned them while General Leslie's Covenanters had simply out-marched them. Following a parallel line on the English right, Leslie had overtaken the English column to gain his position athwart the high road to Berwick, his left with its back to the steep rise of Doon Hill and his right almost down to the sea.

Defeat and surrender confronted the English. Nothing less.

Even under Cromwell's iron hand, supported by Fleetwood, his second-in-command, by John Lambert, his Sergeant Major General, and by Monck himself, the mood of the Army had weakened, perhaps fatally. Few could see a way out of the trap.

During that midnight trudge, it came to Monck with a rueful despair that, once again, despite his personal exertions, he was to be party to military disaster. What its consequences would be for him he dared not consider, but the thought of writing yet another self-exculpatory letter to Anne as some sort of record of what he had achieved was not attractive. The complexities of Ireland had vindicated the first; explaining ill-luck, foul weather and Cromwell's fool-hardy advance offered no attraction in a second. He thought briefly of Anne and then, for a moment, he regarded himself as Jonah, destined to bring ill-luck upon all those with whom he associated. Was it the battering of Battyn that had so excited God against him? Or was it his betrayal of the King's cause? Or, he thought with a spasm of guilt, of the great lie he had told to preserve Cromwell? God, in His omnipotence, knew he could have done little else and that, insofar as he had been able, he had stuck to some semblance of honourable principle in the abominable tangle of this world's dismal affairs. But God made judgements notwithstanding mitigating facts; no doubt poor Judas could advance some excuses for his betrayal of Christ, but look what happened to Judas! And God was undeniably partial; did not the parable of the Prodigal Son prove that? Virtue rested with the steadfast elder brother who had done his duty, but God overset that and prospered the fickle, dissolute and whoring Prodigal. Monck wondered what the psalm-singing Puritan officers of the New Model made of *that*? It was an uncomfortable train of thought and Monck speedily abandoned it.

That afternoon he had met with Cromwell, Fleetwood and Lambert in Dunbar where Oliver had sought the opinion of his most influential senior officers. There was, Cromwell, had said, a hope that they might inflict damage upon Leslie, whose left wing seemed constrained by the steep slope of Doon Hill and the gully through which the burn roared in its angry spate. Both Cromwell and Lambert thought they might turn the enemy's right wing on the lower ground, nearer the sea and thus force the passage through to Berwick. Asked his opinion, Monck did not disagree – it was their only option other than capitulation, a word none could mention – but he held the venture to carry high risk: it was a forlorn hope. But what else could they do? Lambert had asked the question; full of the zeal of the Lord, no doubt, Monck had thought shrugging his shoulders.

His head full of such considerations, Monck leaned into the wind and pressed forward, his staff reluctantly trailing dejectedly in his wake. Then, after ten minutes, he stopped again and one of his followers blundered into him, apologising as he fought to retain his footing in the slippery mire. Monck could hear the breathing of his companions and looked round. What of their faces was revealed beneath the dripping brims of their hats was faint and pallid.

'The rain has eased somewhat,' he remarked, 'and we may make out the lie of the land.' They had topped a low rise, from which the ground fell away slightly. Below them the Broxburn roared its way down to the sea just beyond the front of the English Army, a thin, faintly intermittent white line bounding the darker patches on the grey-black landscape that marked the English soldiers' bivouacs. Only a few hissing fires were visible, the difficulty of finding firewood combining with the rain to render all form of comfort quite impossible.

There was, he thought, a slight lightening of the sky; he looked up, a thinning of the cloud, perhaps? Perhaps not, for it was difficult to determine. The moon should be up, but there was little evidence through the scud. Even so, there, to the right, he could now see the dark, humped loom of Doon Hill reminding him, if he needed it, that Leslie's overwhelming force lay beneath its brow. He scanned the ground that fell away from it to the left, his eye raking the gentle slope beyond the English Army's front and the rushing burn. Here lay the prolonged encampment of the Scots in a line extending from Doon Hill away to the left, where the windswept sea battered the rocky outcrops east of Dunbar. He took his time, sensing the impatience of his companions; for all their wet misery they were eager to roll themselves in their cloaks and lie down under whatever shelter they could find at headquarters. God knew they might even find a bite to eat, left over from the table of the Captain-General, but they were on Monck's staff, worse-luck, and the Lieutenant General commanding the artillery not only had a reputation for diligence beyond the call of duty, but Oliver's wholehearted support. Indeed, it had seemed at times as if Oliver had wearied of his task and resigned himself to all-consuming anxiety, leaving matters of detail to Monck. It was certain that in recent days Cromwell had lost a great deal of his lustre – and no little of his magic either.

Everyone in the English Army knew of the lengths to which Cromwell had gone to secure Monck a regiment of his own. It was the custom in the New Model Army for each field-officer to command his own regiment and Cromwell had to accommodate his new recruit. When the officers and men of what had been Bright's regiment, then quartered at Alnwick, were asked if they would accept Lieutenant General Monck as their Colonel they had objected. 'We captured him at Nantwich!' they had responded dismissively, adding that 'he will betray us.' There were other mutterings, more serious in the God-fearing minds of the Puritan zealots that filled the ranks of the New Model Army; Monck was an adulterous sinner, living in defiance of the Seventh Commandment, contemptuous of the Word of God. He ought, moreover, to have been hanged, for the offence had recently been made capital.

The new colonel appointed to Bright's vacancy was the young and charismatic John Lambert, who was accepted enthusiastically and this completed the structure of the force Parliament had approved for Cromwell's operations against the Scots. Monck was left hanging like a loose stirrup.

Undaunted and determined to both repay Monck the debt he owed him and to establish him in his proper place as Lieutenant General of the artillery (which, without a nominal regiment, was but a cipher in the eyes of the troops), Cromwell had promptly stripped five companies each out of Sir Arthur Haselrig's Blue-Coats at Newcastle and Colonel George Fenwick's newly-raised Northumberland Regiment at Berwick. Both had been appointed to garrison duties and Cromwell's action prised the reluctant soldiers out of their comfortable billets. Of these ten companies he made a regiment for Monck, desiring that Parliament add it to the New

Model's establishment and ordering that the two depleted garrisons be reinforced. Within a fortnight these men had forgotten their billets, forsaken their former identities, to take a new pride in their Colonel for, alone among the high command, Monck was the only professional, and it showed. Monck's ability soon manifested itself, not least by his concern for his men's welfare and by the unremitting demands he made upon himself as much as upon them. Such had been the kernel of his jest with Holmes, who had come to him from Haselrig's Blue Coats. Even amid the present miseries of retreat and entrapment, it was Monck's men who seemed to hold-up best, as they had demonstrated when they had stood so stalwartly against Leslie's cavalry probe the previous night.

Skilled as he was, Cromwell lacked the experience that made of diligence a necessary adjunct to mere command. Lambert was equally handicapped. His abilities as a lawyer competed favourably with his military skills; he was said to be great in council and in the charge of his horsemen, but he relied upon others to attend to the details of commanding the cavalry. The efficient ordering of supplies, even of farrier's stores, seemed beyond Lambert if only he conceived it beneath his dignity. There was, in Monck's opinion, a good too much made of dignity among men of Lambert's stamp. You could only delegate if you understood what was necessary; merely leaving such details to others courted the disaster or negligence, for one failed to spot omissions.

Most, even in that partial army with its fierce and Puritan loyalties, when confronted by the setbacks of the Scottish campaign, perceived virtues in Monck's conduct. Notwithstanding their present predicament, Monck had proved that his was the eye for detail, his the clear and unambiguous order, and his the route of march most advantageous to their progress. Men soon regarded his capture at Nantwich as bad luck, a sticking with his men, rather than taking horse and fleeing. The more perceptive noted with surprise that his method fell-in with that of the New Model Army, causing many to think Monck should have held Lambert's post as Cromwell's chief-of-staff. But the appointment of Lambert had precedence and there was besides the post of second-in-command, a purely political decision settled upon the person of Sir Charles Fleetwood. Reliable, religiously sound, but inexperienced above his regimental command, Fleetwood was no more than a buttress to Cromwell himself. And there were others whose Puritan credentials far outweighed Monck's slender claim to high regard. A cavalryman like Lambert, Colonel Robert Lilburne was also a Regicide, as was Edward Whalley, the Commissary-General of the Horse. Both were fiercely attached to Cromwell, though Lilburne was said to harbour odd political notions like his brother John, the Leveller. Amid this sectarian brotherhood Monck was a parvenu, an older man, experienced but in the eyes of all but Cromwell, unsound, unreliable, a notorious turncoat. Unfazed, Monck quietly undertook many of the duties rightfully Fleetwood's and, more pertinently, Lambert's. It was thus Monck who tended the drudgery of supply, of disposition and of reconnaissance, the subtleties of which his seniors were wont to disregard.

But it began to be bruited abroad that men seemed to turn out of their bivouacs with more fervour if Monck gave the word – second perhaps to Cromwell himself. And it was notable how often it was Monck's regiment that was first to assemble at the muster, or be drawing their stores from the Quartermaster General's train.

For himself, Monck did not care; his devotion to the task was total and if, in doing Lambert's work, Lambert felt slighted, then that was Lambert's problem; Monck knew he had Cromwell's approval and, besides, if he saw to matters himself he was in no doubt but that they were properly accomplished. Lambert was flash-in-the-pan brilliant, but military operations required long hours of dull preparation, and Cromwell knew it. As a mark of his personal faith in Monck, the Captain-General had appointed him the senior of his infantry commanders.

For sure, it had been Monck's guns that had battered the Scots in the opening moves of the campaign, as Cromwell sought to outwit the cunning Leslie before Edinburgh, and it was Monck who, detached from the main force, had taken the fortified houses of Colinton and Redhall. But these were not decisive actions; the nearest they had come to a pitched battle was at Gogar on the Glasgow road where, although within gunshot of each other, the Scots lay on dry ground behind an all but impassable morass. Even Monck had no answer to that.

'Sir, 'tis late …' one of the young gentlemen behind him ventured with a forced cough, prompting him to move on. They were tired and needed rest.

Monck held up his hand; something had caught his eye, in the left distance, on the lower ground beyond the faint line of the rushing burn. 'I think, gentlemen, it is not late, but early. Do you perceive movement? There! Behind the enemy's right?'

There was a moment of silence, as if the young officers could not bring themselves to undertake yet further duty that dismal night. The question seemed to stretch their sense of loyal duty to the utmost.

'Cavalry,' someone said suddenly.

'By God they are extending …' added a second.

'They are advancing their right to envelop our left and will be across the burn to turn our flank,' added the third. 'They will cut us off from the ships!' Apprehension if not fear lent an intensity to the exclamation.

'An encirclement …' the first added almost incredulously, as though the thing were impossible despite the evidence before him.

'Come!' With a sudden movement that, after the havering, surprised his staff, Monck set off at a swift walk towards the small stone farm of Broxmouth House that was Cromwell's headquarters.

As they hastily descended the gentle incline, it began to rain again and the overcast, thick as it was, seemed to increase in density. They passed through the English lines, exchanging password and countersign with the pickets, as the deluge increased. The downpour suppressed the faint snickering from the horse-lines, whence came a farmyard smell redolent of nostalgia for more peaceable times. As they approached

Broxmouth House it was clear the alarm had already been raised. Orderlies gathered about their horses and lantern-light from an open door gleamed in reflection from the churned mud outside the threshold and fell upon the rain glossed flanks of black and bay as they jostled by a stone mounting block. Without ceremony Monck and his party entered the Captain-General's presence, carrying the rain and mud into the candlelit interior.

The handsome Lambert turned and looked-up as Monck entered the crowded room. 'Ah, General Monck,' he said smoothly, 'we were wondering when …'

Monck ignored Lambert's slyly offensive jibe and nodded at the silently anxious Fleetwood. Raking the others with tired eyes he planted his wet gloves on the table and leaned over Cromwell, who, pen-in-hand, was himself bent over a paper. Water from Monck's hat-brim dripped upon the table and Lambert's eyes glittered at the newcomer's effrontery.

'You see where they are moving?' Monck queried abruptly, addressing his remark directly at Cromwell who looked up from the order he was writing.

'I do.' Cromwell gave Monck a wan smile and rose to his feet confronting Monck; it was the signal the group of senior officers had been waiting for and they abandoned their privately muttered conversations and fell silent in anticipation. 'Well?' Cromwell was looking directly at Monck, their faces no more than two feet apart.

'Sir, the Scots have numbers and their hills; these are their advantages. We have discipline and despair, both qualities that will prompt our men to acquit themselves well; these factors are our advantages. My advice is to attack at once.'

Cromwell nodded. 'If we beat the right wing where it stands,' he announced, 'then their whole army is thrashed.' The Captain-General looked round him, his face strained as he bit his lower lip in what had become a compulsive reaction to stress. Monck noted the raw flesh, the bleeding wart; this was a man near the end of his tether.

'Sir Charles?'

'I concur, Sir,' responded Fleetwood with grave obedience.

'General Lambert?'

Lambert's face worked with fury but at Cromwell's demand he answered obediently. 'I too, Sir.'

'General Monck's opinion we already know. Gentlemen …?' Cromwell, looked round the others who muttered their assent. 'Very well, we will make our dispositions accordingly. John,' he turned to Lambert, 'you shall move your horse and Lilburne's across the burn on the left and turn their right flank. Sir Charles will command you.' He looked at Fleetwood then Lilburne who nodded. Turning next to Monck, Cromwell said, 'George, your guns to the front and then wait upon events with your brigade holding the centre …'

'I have a place for guns, Sir,' Monck said quietly.

'Very well,' Cromwell agreed, then continued. 'Colonels Okey and Overton, do you hold the line of the burn. Colonel Pride, I would have your brigade take post in the rear of the horse on the left flank ready to move forward and hold the ground won by Generals Fleetwood and Lambert. That will amount to three regiments of infantry and five of horse mustered on the left. I shall post the reserve …' Cromwell raked them with his bloodshot gaze. 'Any questions?' He paused, then lifted up his eyes to the low, smoke-stained ceiling. 'God is delivering them into our hands, gentlemen. They are coming down to us.'

'May the Lord God of Hosts be praised,' added Fleetwood to a chorus of 'Amens.'

Monck said nothing. Cromwell's fervour stank of desperation.

*

'Up! Up! Up!' Monck waved his hand and then set his shoulder to the wheel of the gun. It was the eighth he had ordered his men to move forward in the hissing darkness of the September night. A chill wind was getting up and might shift the rain-clouds but the sodden ground was almost impassable as they strained at the spokes and thrust the dragging trails through the morass. Only the most vigorous exertions on the part of the artillerymen, their fusiliers and detachments of Monck's regiment detailed to assist, had ensured that within two hours of the order being given, a battery of field guns with its ammunition-laden limbers had been man-handled up to an almost semi-circular bend in the Broxburn which thrust a salient towards the Scots position. From this location, which Monck had earlier marked out, he knew he could both pin-down the Scots centre and prevent a quick reinforcement of the enemy's right from its left flank. In the last hours of the night, as the sky slowly cleared and the moon shone fitfully from behind the streaming clouds, Monck drew up his own brigade in front of Brand's Mill, a little to the left of his guns.

At the head of his troops he accosted an under-officer, Captain Francis Nichols. 'The men have been fed?' he asked brusquely, knowing he had put the matter in train earlier, having ordered what was available from the ships at Dunbar up to the encampment.

'They have sir.'

Monck nodded and turned to the men in their ranks behind Nichols. 'Well, my lads, we shall see what we can do this day,' he said, shouldering his half-pike and walking along their front, his subordinate captains trailing in his wake and each taking his post as they passed their companies. 'You shall show me again of what you are made.'

It was at this point that General Lambert rode up, demanding to speak to General Monck.

'I am here, General Lambert,' Monck identified himself.

'Your guns, General Monck, your guns, they are in the wrong place, sir, kindly move them to where they may be best able to play them upon the enemy's left.'

'My guns are advanced as far as the river, General Lambert, and can enfilade ...'

'They should be more to the right …'

'I know my business sir,' Monck cut in, 'and suggest that you attend to your own which, if I recall it aright, is in command of your cavalry.'

'Have a care, Monck …'

'It is my belief,' Monck went on, seizing Lambert's horse's bridle and tugging its head round, 'that you should be advancing upon the enemy's flank if we are to have the faintest chance of success this day! Good morning to you, General Lambert.' Monck stepped back and slapped his hand upon the rump of Lambert's charger, so that the animal jerked uncertainly and Lambert, in a fury, was obliged to ride off.

'God's wounds,' Monck muttered to himself. 'We do not deserve to be delivered from our present plight.'

Astonishingly, during these active preparations, no sound came from the Scots camp. Masked by the low howl of the wind, the slashing curtains of rain and mist that swept across the low countryside and the rising ground beyond, the English reformed their front from a defensive to an offensive posture while the Scots, having made their own movement to the right in preparation for a morning attack, had lain down to sleep. The wind, though it blew cold in the faces of the English, carried the noise of their manoeuvres away from the enemy. Perhaps God had not entirely deserted them.

As Monck strode along his front, angry at Lambert's presumption and showing himself to his men to stir their blood, he sought to divine their spirit in the pale ovals of their faces, streaked with grime though they were. In the fitful and partial moonlight, he could see, or perhaps he merely sensed, that the call to battle had invigorated them. There was always the other reason, he thought, that death was preferable to the endless marching, squatting and shitting, the poor food and the relentless rain of this God-forsaken land. He kept his exhortations short; it better showed his confidence in them.

'Sir, a bite and some little wine …' Monck turned. A soldier named Rogers, appointed his servant, thrust a crust at him, along with a little cheese and a small flask. Monck thanked him and took the victuals.

'Shall we attack before daylight, General?'

'Overton …' Monck looked up at Colonel Overton who had strolled the length of his own brigade and come upon Monck breaking his fast. 'Yes, we shall, it is our best, indeed, our only chance.' He paused, then asked, 'Your men have been fed?'

'Aye, the Lord be praised, though I know not how the victuals arrived.' Monck said nothing, as Overton added, 'How think you the day will go?'

Monck swallowed the wine which was poor enough stuff, looted no doubt from Broxmouth House. He waved his left hand towards the north, where a thin greyness drew over the distant sea. 'If Fleetwood and Lambert can gain purchase on the left and you can hold them to your front, I think we shall have a chance of pinning them against their hills …'

They were interrupted by a trumpet note that came from the Scots camp. 'The Jockies are awake,' Overton remarked. 'I wish you God's love, General!'

Monck grunted as Overton scrambled back towards his men, his brigade a dark mass against the sodden grass, the pale line of suddenly wavering pike-heads gleaming faintly. Monck wiped his mouth and handed the flask to the silent Rogers. Holmes came up and the two men exchanged a word then Holmes ordered the captains to their posts. Monck picked up his grounded half-pike and walked steadily back to the centre of his own front line. Two of his captains, Nichols and Ethelbert Morgan who commanded the companies in the centre, gathered round him as he lent his weapon upon his shoulder and settled his casque upon his head. Easing his shoulders inside his cuirass he nodded to the north where a movement told where Lambert was on the move at last. Cromwell, would be there and all must await the moment.

'Captain Grove?' Monck called to the officer commanding the battery of guns.

'Sir?'

'Your guns, sir; warn them to make ready and await my order to fire.'

And then he heard it, the faint shout and, looking up, the sudden movement as Lambert's Ironsides, indistinct in the gloom, trotted forward and splashed and plunged across the burn where it ran shallow and wider than it did to Monck's immediate front. The Ironsides were met by a louder shout as the Scots, already under arms, rushed forward to meet the threat. Monck was aware that, as if my some miracle, the sky began to clear. All along the lines, on both sides of the torrent of the burn, there were shouts and acclamations as the Scots sprang to arms. A dozen Scottish standards reared their brazen heads into the moonlight as – at last – the rain petered out. The first gleam of dawn had yet to spread across the field of battle.

Casting his eye to the left and the right, Monck walked forward. He could see Grove a hundred yards away, standing expectantly beside the nearest gun. Monck raised his hand and lowered it smartly; the first discharge boomed out, its ball gouging clods of earth in the very front of Sir James Lumsden's Scots. Monck watched with satisfaction as the enemy line wavered with apprehension. 'Raw troops and they do not like my guns,' he ruminated softly to himself.

Monck was aware of Nichols at the head of his company and just behind the General.

'General Lambert's men make some progress,' Nichols remarked and Monck nodded. To his left he could just make out the red colour of the Ironsides' coats, and the gleam of light upon their steel helmets as they met the Scots cavalry coming down towards them. Monck almost felt the physical shock of the encounter, and sensed the check Lambert sustained as the Scots horsemen, many of them bearing lances, thrust at his Ironsides. Thereafter he paid them no more attention, for the success of Lambert and Fleetwood on the left rested in part upon his own steadfastness in preventing the enemy moving to their right and supporting the Scots horse. Monck walked forward to the guns where Grove was exhorting his artillerymen.

'Play on them, my lads,' Monck shouted in the intervals between two discharges. 'Pin 'em like rats in a trap.' Staring at the burn he thought it unlikely that Lumsden or Innes to his left could cross the torrent without a struggle and, after a few words with the gunners, resumed his position. Calling Nichols and Morgan to him he indicated the flatter land that lay to their left, around Brand's Mill.

'When I give you the order, do you move off and cross the burn there, by the mill. That is where Lumsden will try and strike at us and I would have us meet him halfway.'

'He's on the move, sir,' Nichols remarked. 'I'll be about God's work,' he threw over his shoulder as he trotted off at a loping run, shouting to his company to follow. Monck hefted his pike and turned to look at his men. ‘Make ready!’ he roared and he heard the under-officers passing the order to port their pikes. He could see their faces more clearly now and all in the front rank stared expectantly at him. He grinned at them; what else could he do? Turning about he motioned for the advance. ‘Forward!’

Suddenly there was a young cornet of horse reining-in alongside him, his mount steaming in its exertion, its rider leaning from the saddle.

‘General Monck, sir?’

‘I am he.’

‘General Lambert is checked, sir! The enemy have artillery and infantry behind their horse! The Captain-General desires that you relieve the pressure to your front!’

Monck turned about and waved again to his men. ‘Drummers!’ he yelled before turning to the cornet. ‘I desire that you inform the Captain-General,’ he called out, as the young officer jerked his horse’s head round to the north, ‘that we are already about the day’s business!’

Already the drummers were beating out the order to attack and they were leery at the sharp declivity of the river’s bank.

The Broxburn tore at their legs as they stumbled and waded into its freezing waters. Behind him Monck realised the men, clustered together, derived support from each other whereas he, in the vanguard, several times almost lost his footing, fearful of an ignominious fall under the water’s rush. He was in the burn up to his thighs; then it was up to his waist. He moved one heavy leg forward after the other while leaden balls pinged about them as Lumsden’s musketeers tried enthusiastically to enfilade their advance. Then they were across and, streaming water from their soaked clothing, clambering onto the slippery wet grass and moss on the far bank. This was trampled, squelching, underfoot as, at the words of command, the pike-heads came down and they thrust forward, Monck at their head.

The regiment was out of breath now and Lumsden’s pike-men checked them for twenty long and heaving minutes of thrust, parry and push-of-pike. It was an ugly but familiar business. Monck plied his weapon with an old skill and when it ran through a heavy Scotsman and the press of his fellows behind prevented him extracting it, he let go, drew his sword and laid about him. Caught in the *mêlée* he failed to see what was happening elsewhere, though his brain noted the reassuring thunder of his guns that kept Innes, Piscottie, Holborn and Stewart from coming to Lumsden's aid. At first, though he did not know it until later, Lambert and Fleetwood had been thrown back but, as the daylight increased and Cromwell moved up reinforcements from the reserve, they recrossed the burn and began to roll-up the Scots' right. The enemy, thinking the battle won, had not expected the English to recover so rapidly, or with such a formidably gathering momentum. The bulk of Leslie's infantry now found themselves pinned between the ravine through which the upper Broxburn poured and the rise of Doon Hill, up which, as the daylight grew, Colonel Pride's skirmishers, backed by impetuous horsemen from Lambert's regiments, drove the Scottish cavalry under Browne, Montgomerie, Strachan and Leslie himself. Thus most of those who had first impeded the Ironsides' attack now found the tables turned against them. Pride and the reserve, led by Cromwell himself on a small Scots horse and with his lower lip bleeding from his constant chewing, urged his men to extend to the left, to work their way round the reverse of Doon Hill and come down upon the trapped Scots in the valley of the burn.

In the meantime Monck and his struggling troops had carried Lumsden's position. Lumsden's men had soon begun to give way, falling back before the powerful figure of George Monck, slashing left and right with his sword, leading a steady advance of pike-men supported by galling musketry. Lumsden's inexperienced musketeers had discharged their weapons prematurely and soon ran out of dry powder and shot. Their spare store had been ruined by rain and they began to falter. With his infantry giving ground under Monck's relentless pressure, a mortified and wounded Lumsden was delivered a prisoner into Monck's hands. But Monck now found himself checked, for his regiments discovered themselves confronted by the fresh troops of Sir James Campbell, part of Lawers' brigade drawn up in the rear of Lumsden's crumbling ranks. They proved more stubborn.

Monck's plight was seen by Cromwell who ordered Pride's brigade to his assistance. Led by Cromwell's own regiment, commanded in the field by Lieutenant-Colonel Goffe, Pride's pike-men advanced upon Monck's left, turning Campbell's flank. Slowly the bloody struggle, reduced to push-of-pike and butt of musket as the English pressed up the hill, inclining all the time to the right, always to the right, driving the Scots in upon themselves so that they lost all sense of order. The shouts and roars of enraged men full of blood-lust, the screams of pain and heartless bellows, mixed with the fervid huzzahs of the Godly under the pall of smoke thrown by the artillery, set Monck's teeth on edge as he gasped and fought for a foothold in the slither, calling on his men for ever greater effort in their advance. As Monck's guns in the English centre fell silent for fear of hitting the backs of their own men, so too did those of the faltering, overrun Scots cannon under Doon Hill. There were, as Monck had known, only a handful of these available to Leslie and they presented little threat to the advancing English and a greater danger to the Scots falling back upon them. Pride's intervention, now backed by Lambert and Lilburne's horse which had been reformed after finally throwing back the Scots cavalry, now overran Lawers' brigade and began to roll the entire Scottish force back upon itself, trapping it between burn and hill.

Then up came the sun. 'God's own light thrown across the field of battle,' men said of it afterwards, and the exultations began to sound as the English prevailed against both odds and auguries. Above him Monck could see on the summit of Doon Hill, the red coats of Ironsides. Here and there on the slope were others, small groups wheeling and turning as they hunted out Leslie's broken cavalry from among the whin bushes, while the English infantry completed their encirclement and came down upon the wretched Scotsmen with the wrath of Almighty God and the satisfaction of revenge in their bright and fevered eyes.

Monck's men pressed on. Fighting a desperate rear-guard action, the regiment of Sir John Haldane of Gleneagles was cut to pieces while their fellow countrymen attempted to escape the English onslaught. A bloody Nichols threw three standards at Monck's feet and a badly wounded Scots captain fell on his knees, giving up his sword in return for quarter and his life. Somewhere a cavalry trumpet sent out the faint notes for a rally and then Monck heard it, the noise of the New Model Army at worship. Faint at first, but ever stronger as the fight in his immediate vicinity began to falter and fade, and the enemy fell like sheaves of wavering corn, came to him the words of the One-hundred and seventeenth Psalm.

'Oh, praise the Lord all ye heathen: Praise him all ye nations.

For His merciful kindness is ever more and more towards us:

And the truth of the Lord endureth for ever. Praise the Lord.'

As Monck leaned, panting, upon his sword, regarding the shattered enemy ranks and the dreadful slaughter about him, he heard a second trumpet, this time sounding the advance. Cromwell, full of the zeal of the Lord of Hosts, pressed the cavalry onwards in pursuit, harrying the fleeing Scots. Those of Leslie's army not at the feet of the English begging for their lives, streamed back the way both armies had come, past Bellhaven and Haddington, opening the road to Edinburgh.

All thought of that to Berwick was now forgotten. This was no longer a retreat.

*

'See, General Monck, a score of enemy standards, three thousand prisoners…'

If Lambert's extravagant gesture at the Scots colours leaning against the wall in Broxmouth House was in some way meant as an admonishment to Monck, it foundered on his well-known taciturnity. Monck forbore any comment and, ignoring Lambert entirely, advanced to the table where Cromwell sat, as he had sat in the small hours, composing his despatch for Parliament. This time he removed his hat.

'It has pleased Almighty God to give us the victory. Make arrangements to march on Edinburgh immediately,' the

Captain-General said without looking up. Monck turned his head towards Lambert, acknowledging Cromwell's order but making it clear that he would carry out what Lambert should have already undertaken.

'It is in hand, sir,' he said quietly. 'Do I understand that General Lambert commands the pursuit?'

Cromwell bit his lower lip and looked up, first at Monck and then at Lambert. 'It is the Lord's work, gentlemen, kindly be about it with all speed. Let us not throw away what advantage God has granted us, His name be praised.'

'Amen to that,' Monck responded with a hint of irony, staring at Lambert's flushed face. Without a word, the younger man stamped out of the room.

Monck was in the act of following him when, without lifting his head, Cromwell said, 'He is young George, and his impetuosity carried the day.' Monck held his tongue, divining the line the Captain-General was taking in apportioning credit for the victory in the despatch he was composing for the benefit of London. That much was to be expected, he thought, as he made a second attempt to leave, but the Captain-General looked up and added, 'as did thy steadfastness, George.'

Monck made a small bow before withdrawing. Outside in a thin and watery sunshine his orderly held his horse's bridle. Just then John Okey's dragoons approached and their commander saluted him. 'Onwards to Edinburgh, General Monck!' he called cheerfully.

'God speed you, Colonel Okey!' Monck responded, suddenly aware that this was a moment to savour, like the breach at Breda.

Surely their fortunes had turned upon a whim of fate. Or perhaps God *had* willed it, after all, for it was whispered among the men that that day was the Captain-General's birthday. Characteristically Monck cast aside the philosophical train of thought; there was work to be done and, in his experience at least, God helped those who helped themselves.

SCOTLAND

September 1650 – February 1652

It may have been the flurry of hailstones that beat like a snare-drum upon the small windows of the governor's apartment in Edinburgh Castle, or it may have been the slight commotion in the antechamber that roused Monck from his concentration on the papers before him. The list of requisitions would have distracted a less diligent man hours ago, but the distraction was, nevertheless, almost welcome. He looked first at the window, the view from which he was familiar with, seeing the flattening of the chimney-smoke over the crowded roofs of the city as the squall swept in from the north-west.

'Summer,' he muttered with a mild, half-amused contempt.

But it was the commotion in the antechamber that revealed itself as the source of disturbance as the intervening door was flung open and the small, irrepressible figure of Lieutenant Colonel Thomas Morgan burst into the room with Monck's frustrated secretary, William Clarke, making apologetic gestures behind him.

'Colonel Morgan!' Monck exclaimed, rising to his feet, his smile genuine as he greeted his companion in arms.

'Lieutenant General Monck,' Morgan responded with a flourish of mock gravity that bespoke an understanding born of friendship between the two men. 'I have news, sir …'

'Of Lambert?' Monck asked anxiously, aware of the attack David Leslie had mounted from his position at Torwood.

'Indeed. And a brilliant affair it was too,' Morgan admitted, well aware of the antipathy between Lambert and Monck. But Monck was too seasoned a campaigner to concern himself with belittling Lambert's success; it mattered to Monck only that he had *been* successful and Morgan knew it. 'He acted with consummate skill,' the little Welshman said, 'hiding the bulk of his force behind a reverse slope and then falling upon the enemy's right flank.'

'He has a genius for such tactical flourishes,' Monck conceded admiringly.

'They say two thousand men were killed in half an hour,' Morgan went on, 'fourteen hundred Jockies, no less, have been taken prisoner and Sir John Browne, their captain, has been wounded, mortally it is feared.' Morgan smiled. '*In summa*, sir, we finally hold the north bank of the Forth.'

Morgan did not need to add that this news would be more than welcome to Monck. Since Dunbar the victors' fortunes had not waxed without intermittent disappointment. It was true that, in addition to those felled or captured upon the field of battle, the pursuit that followed the slaughter had yielded a further four thousand dead and eight thousand prisoners; but David Leslie had escaped to Stirling with five thousand men and immediately reformed the Covenanters' army with great skill and in short order. And all the while his moss-troopers had continued to harry the English whenever and wherever possible, interdicting the desperately needed convoys of food-wagons sent up from Newcastle and Berwick. Moreover, although in the aftermath of Dunbar Lambert's cavalry had taken Edinburgh, the citadel itself had defied capture. Cromwell, his main army riven with sickness, had failed to seize Stirling wherein Leslie held out, forcing the Captain-General to fall back upon Linlithgow where he entrenched himself. Here, he too had succumbed to a fever.

It was left to Monck and Lambert to systematically reduce the moss-troopers' strongholds throughout that bleak November, striking hither and yon to the discomfiture of the Scots. It had meant hard riding in continuing foul weather, and the motivating of a tired soldiery that faltered from exhaustion and the desire to retire into winter quarters.

'I thought this the New Model,' Monck was fond of growling at its disaffected officers in an attempt to encourage them to ever greater efforts. As for himself, he appeared everywhere with a relentless energy that could not fail to impress. Even Lambert commented upon it.

In addition to his near-demonic descents upon outpost and encampment alike, Monck fostered another form of warrior from among the prisoners taken at Dunbar. Setting up a tent and with Will Clarke in close attendance, Monck fell to interviewing Scotsmen of all sorts. His persuasions, argued in a reasonable tone and larded with references to the will of Almighty God and for the good of all God-fearing men, were further augmented by a judicious disbursement of silver coin and the promise of more. It was sufficient to turn some men Judas and convert others into reliable intelligencers. Such men learned to answer to Will Clarke, head of Monck's Intelligence Department, who reported to his master.

The swift descents of Lambert's cavalry upon assemblies of Covenanters whenever word came in of their doings from these newly recruited spies began to sap the enemy's will and enabled Monck to bring up his guns wherever the Scots took shelter behind stone walls. The appearance of Monck's cannon so intimidated the garrison of Dirleton Castle, a fortress a few miles from the field of Dunbar, that it begged for quarter. Soon afterwards his artillery had similarly reduced Roslin and Borthwick castles; word of Monck as a force to be reckoned with spread through the lowland valleys.

But there were harder nuts to crack and when Monck turned his attention to Edinburgh Castle it seemed that his run of luck was over. He sent for miners from Derbyshire who dug under the looming spurs of jutting rock upon the summit of which the mighty fortress squatted. Into their under-mining he packed quantities of fine-milled gunpowder and set a spark to the train therefrom. The resulting explosions blew tons of granite in the faces of the besiegers, killing a score or so, but effecting little against the castle which continued to hold-out under its governor, Walter Dundas.

In the meanwhile Monck had summoned heavy siege guns which were brought up to Leith by sea. These he had laid with great deliberation and the assistance of his engineer, one Joachim Hane, on the ramparts of the citadel. Intermittently throughout the day – for they were slow to load – the heavy crump of this monstrous artillery could be heard, gradually wearing down both the stonework of the castle's outer works, but also the morale of those inside it.

Finally, hearing of Lambert's defeat of a relieving force of Covenanters under Ker, and fearing the further effects of Monck's heavy cannon which were proving effective in their work of demolition, Dundas capitulated on Christmas Eve. Monck had marched in to take possession of the fortress that dominated the Scots capital and, no more than an hour later, had received by galloper Cromwell's commission appointing him governor of the city.

Monck was too phlegmatic and experienced a campaigner to have his head turned by this elevation. Taking up his quarters in Dundas's old chambers he took stock. There would be no return to Anne for some time, as he had briefly written to her, for there remained much to do. The chief concern of the English was the destruction of the Covenanters main force, growing by the day and for which invaders must cross the Firth of Forth.

Mustering troops in considerable numbers at Leith, early in the New Year, an embarkation was ordered into an assembly of boats from the fleet which had now come up from the south and was anchored in Leith Road. Pulling gallantly in windy conditions, the fleet's oarsmen had all but accomplished the four-mile crossing to the north shore at Burntisland, when a savage and accurate fire from the Scots' guns threw them back. But it had not only been the enemy that had foiled the attempt. That the boats had only narrowly escaped wholesale capsize in the chop thrown up by the wind and tide in the firth was a salutary lesson to their commander; in future, tidal water would be an element to respect.

Discouraged from a further attempt on the Fife shore until the weather moderated, a disappointed Monck took heart from another opportunity. In conference with the fleet's commander, Richard Deane, he accepted Deane's offer of the use of his ships for shore bombardment. In February, further encouraged by the disorder in the countryside and the beneficial consequences of his liberality to informers, Monck resumed his counter-harrying of the moss-troopers' lairs. He had moved the artillery train east, towards Tantallon Castle where, within forty-eight hours, helped by the guns of Deane's men-of-war anchored offshore, Monck's six huge siege-guns had battered a breach in the great curtain wall across the promontory upon which Tantallon perched. Monck had then used a heavy mortar to throw explosive carcasses into the bailey to intimidate the garrison with such effect that the fortress soon fell.

Word of this travelled fast, seemingly born upon the wings of the hooded crows and jackdaws that the concussion of the artillery scared from their roosts in the ramparts of Tantallon. It had only remained for Monck to move west again, and order his great guns to open fire upon Blackness Castle - not far from Oliver at Linlithgow - for the enemy to be cleared out of the area south of the Forth. Buoyed up by this success, and urged on by Deane, in whom he found a friend and a collaborator, Monck next made another attempt to cross the Forth.

At Deane's suggestion he had some weeks earlier ordered the construction of a number of flat-bottomed boats, an undertaking that had been completed by April. Monck now ordered a second attack on Burntisland. Again the firth proved a difficult obstacle and the defenders too determined. The boats had once more returned to the safety of Leith harbour, the troops disembarking in dismay and frustration, eyes cast down as they passed Monck who moved among them, speaking encouragingly. Few met his eyes, for all were crestfallen; the New Model was losing its faith in the God of Battles, and perhaps in General Monck.

But by now Oliver had recovered from his fever and sought to breathe new life into his demoralised soldiery. Word reached Monck that the Captain-General had again taken the field in an attempt to discomfit Leslie and bring the reinvigorated Covenant Army to battle. Monck was ordered to cause a diversion by taking Callendar House, near Falkirk, but to his fury this cost him losses in officers and men from his own regiment. Meanwhile a further attempt was made to cross the Forth, not at Burntisland, but higher, where the river was narrower, between North and South Queensferry. By 18 July a small force of English under Overton had advanced into the Kingdom of Fife and lay at Inchkeithing, whereupon Lambert was hard on Overton's heels, crossing the firth to increase the English strength and – at last – alarming Leslie.

Despatching four thousand men under Sir John Browne to dislodge the invaders, Leslie retained his main force at Torwood. Perhaps, in not sending more, or of accompanying the detachment himself, Leslie was overconfident, but he was no longer in supreme command of the Scots. For months, including the weeks of the Dunbar campaign, his actions had been subject to a council comprised chiefly of Kirk Elders, limiting the scope of Leslie's authority. Now worse was imposed upon him, for the youthful King Charles II – acknowledged the rightful King of Scotland - had assumed the role of commander-in-chief and Leslie's influence waned still further.

For Charles it was not Scotland – whose support he had gained by compromise – that formed the royal objective, but England and its vacant, dispossessed throne.

While Lambert had moved across the Forth, Monck had returned to Edinburgh Castle, anxious as ever about the supplies without which nothing could function and Lambert would most certainly founder. These had assumed a greater urgency and importance than the spies' reports that Will Clarke collected among the taverns of the city. It was therefore in the castle, fretting over the delays in the despatch of powder and flints from Berwick and concerned at the arrival of ships coming north from the Thames laden with military necessities that Morgan had found Monck.

After accepting a glass of wine, Morgan reached for his satchel and took from it a sealed paper. 'I bring orders from the Captain-General,' he said, handing the document to Monck, who swiftly opened the seal. 'Oliver is in a lather to get our main force across the Forth in support of Lambert …'

'And wishes me to secure Burntisland harbour,' said Monck, his eyes scanning Cromwell's written instruction.

'I have already ordered the boats downstream from Queensferry to Leith,' Morgan said. 'You could embark in the morning.'

'Very well,' Monck replied, looking at Clarke, who hovered in the doorway. The secretary nodded and then withdrew. 'That should draw Leslie eastwards,' he added, addressing Morgan.

The Welshman nodded. 'Oliver will get the battle he wishes for to finally despatch the Covenanters.'

'Let us hope so.' Monck sat and reached for quill and paper. 'Do you make everything ready at Leith, Tom. I must pass word for the artillery to embark, and move the infantry at my disposal by first light.' He was already bending over the paper, his pen busily scratching its imperatives across it, as Morgan, tossing off his glass of wine, acknowledged his instructions. He left Monck at his desk, sealing his orders before passing them to his secretary for an orderly to carry to others.

*

On 24 July 1651 Monck's forces had captured the little island of Inchgarvie, which lay midway across the Firth of Forth, before reaching the north bank. On the 29th his men had moved downstream and taken Burntisland itself; then, as July ended, Cromwell's main forces from Linlithgow finally crossed the Forth *en masse*, by way of the safe-haven of Burntisland harbour.

All was now in giddy motion; by 2nd August the English Army in Scotland had marched north, traversing the isthmus of the Fife peninsula, reaching the banks of the Tay and compelling the surrender of Perth. Cromwell let it be known that he intended halting Leslie to the south-east of the city and bringing him to a decisive battle; troops, guns, ammunition were moved up with all despatch so that all was set for such a bloody encounter. But Oliver was deceived; instead of smashing the Covenanters, the Captain-General received unwelcome intelligence from his own scouts and Monck's Scottish spies. Leslie had abruptly halted his advance, then turned back for Stirling. It took a day before this astonishing news was confirmed; Monck's agents reporting that upon hearing Cromwell's advance northwards across Fife, King Charles had ordered Leslie to join him.

'Oliver has been cheated of his pell-mell battle,' Monck remarked to Clarke as he drew up an order for the morrow. 'But I sense we have to hand the climax of affairs.'

An hour later, as Monck dined with a handful of his staff officers, Clarke announced the arrival of a galloper. The messenger brought Monck a peremptory summons to Cromwell's headquarters at Kinross, south of Perth. Here, on the 3 August 1651, the Captain-General called a Council of War.

Leaning forward over a paper-strewn table, Cromwell stared in turn at the faces of his assembled field-officers.

'Charles Stuart marches south,' he said, pausing to allow the import of his words sink in. 'Reinforced by Leslie, he essays the invasion of England by way of the west coast, no doubt intending to recruit from those in the north-west of England and Wales still adhering to his party.' Oliver straightened up, lightly brushing his hands, as if unconcerned with any possibilities that might arise from this bold and potentially consequential act.

''Tis a folly; a desperate gambit. True, he seeks to deceive us, to march south and raise the country while our main army is occupied in Scotland.' Again he raked his commander's faces, his own set firm, his tone purposeful. 'I doubt that he will reach London,' Cromwell remarked with prescient confidence, 'as Harrison lies at Carlisle at the head of three thousand men and I have requested the Council of State to assemble a further force at Chester.' The Captain-General fell silent as his audience stirred, giving low voice to its reaction to the news.

'Black Tom will not suffer this to go unchallenged,' Lambert remarked with easy familiarly, referring to Sir Thomas Fairfax who, rather than fight the Scots, had retired to his estate in Yorkshire when Parliament offered him command of the Army.

'No,' agreed the Captain-General, 'I am certain that Sir Thomas will not suffer any of this and will surely be moved to call out the Yorkshire levies. Moreover, I mean to inform Mr Speaker Lenthall that although the Scots are embarked upon a descent on London, which may trouble some men's thoughts and cause us a measure of inconvenience – we being some days in their rear – nevertheless, the Lord shall bring us up with them and show them the folly of their desire.'

'Amen to that,' someone murmured and was met with a murmur of agreement. But not everyone considered Oliver's confidence to be justified and there was a nervous atmosphere in the Council, an anxiety to be off in hot pursuit. Cromwell ignored the doubting Thomases and, looking briefly around the assembled officers, divining their concern. 'We shall, of course, with God's good grace, undertake the pursuit and destruction of the Scots but it will be to no avail if the Malignant's son escapes us and returns hither. He will yet command unconditional support from the Highlands and we shall have our work here to do all over again.'

This was better; the attending officers nodded their agreement in their eagerness not to delay. 'I have it therefore in mind to divide our forces. General Lambert will lead the pursuit and General Monck, with those regiments still recruiting their strength, will remain in Scotland.' Cromwell looked up at Monck. 'I shall leave the siege train in your hands, with the greater part of the artillery. Leslie has too little to cause us any fear in this regard and we shall move faster without encumbrance. Do you therefore take Stirling without delay and thereafter act as you think best; with Stirling in our hands much good fortune may follow.'

'Aye sir.' Monck acknowledged the order. 'And those regiments you intend to leave …?'

Cromwell referred to a paper Monck himself had drawn up several days earlier. 'Of foot, three: your own, along with Colonel Reade's and Colonel Ashfield's; of horse four, those of Colonels Hacker, Okey, Alured and Grosvenor; you will also have several troops of dragoons, which I have yet to determine, and two companies of fire-locks to guard the artillery train. In all some five thousand men …' Cromwell looked up at Monck, his sentence unfinished, expecting Monck to solicit more.

Monck nodded. 'That should suffice, sir, if you consider you have sufficient to settle affairs with Leslie.' Monck, aware of Lambert's close scrutiny, avoided any mention of the enemy commander-in-chief, Charles Stuart.

'I shall, of course, request the Council of State reinforces you.'

Monck nodded again, acquiescing gracefully. With a hostile army marching upon them, he could not see the Council stirring themselves greatly on behalf of an army detachment left five hundred miles away, especially as it was left under the command of that former royalist, George Monck. Lambert caught his eye and Monck read the same thoughts in the expression of the man he had come to see as his rival. In Lambert's perception this was an added disincentive, with the army detachment in question under the command of a man whose personal loyalty to the Parliament had yet to be tested. Oliver, it was clear Lambert thought, took a great risk in leaving Scotland in Monck's hands. But then Lambert was unaware of the great debt Oliver owed Monck. Nor could Lambert possibly know with what relief Monck – fully aware of all of this, not least of Oliver's testing trust - grasped his opportunity.

Later that day, knowing a courier would depart for London before the army divided next morning, he dashed off a letter to Anne.

I am left Governor of Scotland, my dearest, he wrote, adding without any thought for material gain, but only that of reputation,

and if God wills it, we should prosper from this providential circumstance. The delay in the settlement of our own affairs may seem hard to bear but I beg you to be patient as I believe it to conduce to a happy and untrammelled outcome.

With her good sense Anne would divine his meaning. He enclosed a brief note for William Morrice, who had agreed to take over the greater part of the administration of his affairs, asking Anne to forward it, then sat back, allowing his thoughts to drift south, to dwell a moment upon his private life, before giving his whole attention to the task he had been set.

*

The day after the army had divided, as Monck's detachment broke camp, orders were received from Cromwell to send Colonel Hacker's regiment to join him. 'I send you Colonel Berry's that you be not further weakened,' the Captain-General wrote in a hastily scribbled note. In taking his departure, Hacker had remarked with a smile that, 'I know not where lies the greater glory, sir, but am sorry to leave you.'

Monck conceded his slow smile, reaching up to clasp Hacker's hand as the other leant over his saddle-bow. 'If the Captain-General catches the enemy there is no doubt of that, if not matters will fall out God-knows how. Here we have ordinary work to do,' he said releasing Hacker's hand.

'God grant you every success, General Monck.' With a salute Hacker turned his horse, and trotted after his men the dust of whose march was already being flattened by an onset of mizzling rain.

Monck watched him go then turned aside to find Okey and Alured awaiting his order to move their cavalry off towards Stirling, the advance guard of his little army. He caught an exchange of glances between them and knew its import. They too had their suspicions about Monck, and they lay not just with doubts as to his loyalty. His abilities in plain soldiering were manifest enough; not a man in the army would doubt that, but the organisation of logistics was a boring, if necessary, business, an affair best left to a man of dull and stolid worth, a man of proven ability to cope with so turgid a preoccupation. How, that anxious exchange of glances revealed, was such a fellow going to cope with independent command and matters of manoeuvre? It was, after all, Lambert who had succeeded in crossing the Firth of Forth.

And not just independent command of a corps ancillary to the main force, but one left in its rear, in occupation of an entire and hostile country? Both Alured and Okey – and presumably all their fellow colonels left under Monck's command – would rather have been riding south with Oliver, whatever fate had in store for the Captain-General. Well, he thought, as the mizzle turned into a fine rain, he would have to show them that Honest George was not quite the dullard they supposed.

'Very well, gentlemen,' he said with a smile, 'do you move your horse off. I shall send the artillery and the bulk of the infantry after you and await only Colonel Berry before I follow.' Both officers raised their right hands to their hats and were about to pull their horses heads round when he added, 'there may be little glory here,' he said indicating the rain with a rueful expression, 'but I intend to finish the labour of conquering Scotland before the winter sets in. I rely upon you to play your part, and with vigour, gentlemen, with vigour. Nothing less, mark you.'

The two cavalrymen exchanged a further intimate glance as they muttered their acknowledgement of Monck's command. He watched them as they rode off, Alured at a dashing canter, Okey at a slower trot.

'They'll see, George, they'll see,' muttered Morgan, who had come up quietly and stood by Monck's side, invested with his new responsibilities as Monck's chief-of-staff. Monck turned and looked at the Welshman.

'Beware insubordination, Tom,' he growled.

'I have no fear of thy fair-mindedness, General Monck,' Morgan said in a low voice, tinged with companionable irony.

'Nor I of thy loyalty, Colonel,' Monck responded with mock hauteur. The two men exchanged grave smiles. 'Now, let us move this rabble forward and take Stirling!'

'Amen to that.'

*

On the 6th Monck's little army lay encamped before Stirling, whereupon he summoned the garrison and the town, promising freedom from plunder or violence. The town clerk and several senior citizens approached after some hours' wait, during which threats of storming the town coerced the city fathers into submission. The delay afforded every opportunity for those disinclined to treat with the enemy to retire into the castle from which no reply was received and was therefore deemed to be in defiance.

At one o'clock in the morning following, Monck's troops marched into Stirling and were billeted on the townsfolk; they were under strict orders to conduct themselves properly and such was the discipline in the detachment of the New Model Army under General Monck that matters passed off peacefully enough. The castle was another matter, as was the surrounding countryside. Unwilling to allow the population to think that by sitting down with his guns in front of Stirling Castle, Monck intended ignoring the rest of the country, he sent a column north, to pass over the mountains and harry remnants of the Covenant Army left behind by King Charles and Leslie. This move was unexpected, both by friend and foe alike, for the column included artillery sent to traverse country over which no field-gun – not even the light leather-guns Monck despatched – had ever been seen in so hostile a terrain. Only Morgan was unsurprised.

On the 7th the proper investment of Stirling Castle began, with wooden platforms under construction for the siege-guns then being brought upstream. These included two heavy mortars, capable of throwing charged and fused carcasses over the walls, where their explosions would burst them asunder, throwing the fragments of their cases hither-and-thither, to the very great terror of those within the walls. Other guns were mounted in vantage points in the town, several small pieces being hoisted into the steeple of the church, from where they could play with advantage upon the ramparts of the castle's outer ward. Four days later all was in place and the bombardment began in earnest, the mortars being supervised by Monck's specialist, the pyroballogist Joachim Hane.

Despite Hane's expertise, Monck was everywhere at once, directing the artillery, encouraging Hane's men, placating the town's councillors and reassuring the population as the thunder of his cannon and mortars shook the houses of the citizens to their foundations. The protestations at the use of the church were silenced when the garrison began to fire upon the steeple and struck it several times. Meanwhile, although the more serious business of investigating the citizen's complaints of plundering and drunkenness among his troops he left to his provost marshal, Monck did not neglect the consequences of this officer's findings. Nor did he scruple to order severely condign punishments – by way of public floggings – to be inflicted upon five of Colonel Berry's men who were convicted of straggling and plundering. One, whose offence had been that of robbery, was shot by order of the General, the first manifestation of Monck's ruthless but lawful governance. He also removed all of Berry's men from their comfortable billets in the town, sending them to bivouac in the surrounding countryside, a collective punishment designed to impress the townsfolk as much as to remind the disaffected soldiery that they were now under George Monck's command. As might be expected, this did not go unnoticed elsewhere in the ranks, but nor was its import entirely ignored by the Scots wronged by the action of the condemned man and his fellow malefactors.

After three days of bombardment with Hane's mortars whose shells burst with intimidating as much as material effect and during which the castle's governor, Colonel William Conyngham, refused every summons of Monck's, there came rumours that the garrison were in a mutinous state. No-one knew how such news passed from the castle's fastness to the besieging force, but these intimations took form when a drummer appeared on the ramparts to beat a parley. He was said by an observer standing nearby to be a highlander from his attire. Hane ceased his fire and this then slackened all along the line. Called to the church's steeple Monck levelled his glass at the drummer, pointed out to him by Hane.

'He's a highlander, sir,' remarked Hane. 'I understand them to be a wild breed, noted for their unreliability. Ahh, see there …'

Monck observed the man seized by others and dragged down from his conspicuous position. Clearly opinion was divided within the fortress but, an hour or so later, an officer emerged with authority to treat for a capitulation. Monck acceded.

Monck agreed that Conyngham and his men might march out with their colours flying. He need not have given such generous terms and overheard Colonel Okey say as much the following day, whereupon he upbraided the cavalry officer.

'But, sir,' Okey responded with that freedom of opinion that Monck had learned came easily to officers of the New Model Army, 'we shall only have to defeat them anew when next we encounter them.' The sentiment roused a rumble of agreement from other officers then within Monck's headquarters, so that he looked up and took them all in at a glance.

'Do not mistake me, gentlemen,' he said firmly, 'and see this as a weakness, but as an augmentation of our position. What Colonel Okey says is incontrovertible. We shall surely meet these fellows again – but consider what we have gained. The way is now open to us to advance further; the enemy's main power is in England, the remnant of his forces left in Scotland is now wary of our puissance and these fellows who march out so boldly were as much destroyed by their own disloyalty in a mutiny as by our artillery. True, they will console themselves with their survival, but we have the measure of them and, in marching out they despoiled some of their fellow-countrymen who are now the better inclined to submit to our government, providing it is maintained with scruple under the rule of law. Thus, Colonel Okey is correct, in a strictly military sense, as he should be as a colonel of horse.'

Monck looked at the half-moon of faces, unaware that their opinion of him was undergoing transformation, and went on: 'For my part, gentlemen, the matter is of greater moment. That handful of liberated men are better employed spreading the word of our victory among their fellows, admitting by their presence their own failure and thus relieving us of the obligation to quarter, guard and feed them.' He paused, looking about him. 'Have you anything more to say upon the subject, Colonel Okey?'

'Nothing, sir,' said Okey, his face downcast.

'I do not rebuke you, Colonel,' Monck said, looking from the dejected Okey to the wider circle of attending officers, 'but I shall not explain myself twice.' Monck paused a moment before continuing. 'And now, let us settle the matter of the garrison and the orders for the route of march for the morrow

…' He gestured to the attending Clarke and, as that worthy dipped his quill, began to issue his orders. 'Colonel Alured, you will lead the advance and command the vanguard …'

Although Monck's army had not pillaged Stirling castle, being rewarded by a distribution of disposable booty, his power was augmented by the capture. Three heavy iron and twenty brass guns, eleven of the light, highly mobile leather-bound cannon were seized, along with twenty-six barrels of black-powder, reels of slow-match, shot and small-arms ball all fell into English hands, besides rundlets of claret and two score barrels each of beef and beer. In addition to these necessaries, Monck took possession of an earl's coronet, his robes and sundry tapestries, all of which he sent off in the shallop which had brought the mortars up the Forth to tranship for London at Leith.

The surrender of the castle marked the end of Monck's obligations to Cromwell; hereafter the six thousand men under his command were at his own disposal, subject to his own plan of campaign for the reduction of Scotland.

Sending some of his heavy siege artillery back to Edinburgh by water, a week after taking Stirling, Monck marched out of the town. The majority of the horse led, followed by the main column, the vanguard consisting of Berry's and Grosvenor's foot while Monck followed Ashfield's infantry with the artillery train, three so-called 'battering pieces' and one mortar. Behind this came Monck's own regiment, the rear being covered by Colonel Okey's horsemen.

Monck's line of march led first towards Dunblane, then, with the Ochill Hills rising to the right, alongside the sparkling river through Strathallan towards Blackford. Beyond, near St Johnston's, his army bivouacked in open country on the 23rd. That evening, as Monck sat down at their mess with his senior officers in a small, requisitioned farmhouse whose occupants watched fearfully as the English officers quartered themselves in their yard, an orderly brought a stranger in.

'Captain Nehemiah Bourne, General Monck,' the stranger introduced himself, 'commander of the man-o'-war *Speaker*, of the third-rate, lately come south from my station on the

Tay.' Bourne cheerfully added, 'where I sent some shot into Dundee to stir the Jocks up. I also laid my guns on St Andrew's and sent them a summons by way of an obliging fisherman, promising them a visitation from your army if they did not comply.' Bourne's chirpiness was catching, and several of those present laughed at the naval commander's effrontery.

'That was well done, sir,' responded Monck, 'though I was not intending to invest St Andrew's.'

'So I judged, sir, but I thought it none the less wise to set the wind at their deliberations,' Bourne replied, not a whit dismayed.

'You rode from Burntisland?'

'Aye, sir, and with the news that biscuit, cheese and other provender for your troops is on its way.' Bourne was now serious. 'You are for Dundee, I think. That is where the Scots presently fasten their seat of government.'

'So I hear, Captain Bourne, and you are for your supper, no doubt. Please,' Monck waved at the end of the table, motioning an orderly to find a chair, plates and cutlery for the visitor, 'do you join us.' They resumed the meal and, after a few moments' thought Monck looked at Bourne. 'In view of what you have said, Captain Bourne, I think we ought to send a summons to St Andrew's.'

Bourne, who was chewing vigorously on a large slice of mutton, nodded vigorously, swallowed hurriedly and added, 'I promised protection and free-trade, sir, if that …'

'Yes, that is entirely in accord with my objective. Let us move the army across the river towards Perth tomorrow and then consider St Andrew's.'

On the following day the advance continued as Monck forced his troops onwards. In late August the weather was fair, the roads, such as they were, were passable and the countryside sufficiently cowed to pose no threat. Monck had had sufficient experience of rain and wind not to waste the clemency of the elements. They crossed the Earn without mishap but, bereft of boats, the Tay east of Perth posed a problem and they did not pass it without casualties. Four men and as many horses were lost to the river as Monck sent most of Alured's cavalry and the dragoons ahead to clear the route towards Dundee, ordering a single troop of Alured's horse to St Andrew's with his summons. Under Monck's impatient impetus, the main army followed, reaching Beligarney that night; there remained only a day's march to Dundee.

The next morning, accompanied by several officers, Monck rode forward to join Alured. Colonel Matthew Alured was a fanatical Anabaptist, a man reborn in Christ Jesus who applied this invigoration to the pursuit of his craft: a commander of cavalry. Like so many of his fellow New Model Army colonels, Alured derived his professional drive not from a pure dedication to soldiering, as did Monck, but from the conviction that he did God's work on earth and was thus an instrument of the Almighty. Imbued with such a numinous motive Alured was, like Lambert, always keen to prove the superiority of his method over the dogged plodding of the old soldiers of fortune who, to many of the officers of the New Model, raised by necessity and a smiling fortune, were not as good as they thought themselves. In pursuit and battle Alured and his fellows had a point; they excelled where sudden and determined action was needed, such was required of a Christian soldier, but war was not all about pursuit and battle and while he rode headlong towards Dundee, Monck and his entourage riding hard to catch up with him, Alured dreamed of appearing before the city and striking fear into the heart of its defenders so that they lay down their arms upon the instant. How could they not, for he had God at his saddle-bow?

Despite Bourne's brief bombardment of the city, a small but potent symbol of the long arm of English power, a rumour was rife that King Charles had already gained a victory over his enemies in England. Thus it was that when Alured thundered up to the city gates they were flung shut in his face and his summons was turned off with derision. His pride pricked and God insulted, Alured was less than pleased to greet Monck who also sent word forward, only to receive the same rebuff. Worse, the governor of Dundee, Sir Robert Lumsden, convinced of Charles's turn of fortune and Monck's rashness, ordered Monck himself to lay down his arms and seek enlistment in the King's service, 'In which you so lately distinguished yourself.'

Having read Lumsden's missive Monck spared no more than a contemptuous glance at his emissary, leaving Alured to chivvy him back whence he came, while he himself rode back along the line of advance to encourage the artillery train and its escort of trudging fusiliers forward at its best speed. Watching the crest-fallen Alured display his frustration, Monck issued a series of orders as his regiments came up. He had been alerted by his spies that a mere fourteen miles away, in the small town of Alyth lying under a shoulder of the Grampian Mountains, the Scottish Committee of Estates and an assembly of military officers had gathered to decide how to counter the movements of the remnant of the English army left in Scotland. After a brief conference with Clarke and Morgan, Monck ordered another of his flying-columns to make themselves ready.

Besides English troops, he included a group of Scots deserters and ordered his own men to attire themselves as like the Scots as possible. Choosing Morgan to lead this odd detachment, supported by the restless Alured, Monck despatched it to Alyth without delay. Hoping thereby to catch the Scots hierarchy by surprise, he turned his own attention back to Dundee.

These bold moves might have mighty consequences, but there were other matters to concern him. The news that the shallop taking the mortars downstream from Stirling had sunk thanks to the excessive weight of her cargo displeased Monck greatly but there was little he could do about it. Of greater importance was the concentration of his army. The speed of his advance from Stirling had meant that many of his soldiers had straggled and that evening he passed a general order by galloper back down the line of advance that on pain of death all should muster to their respective colours without delay. So solidly established was his reputation that this admonition brought the laggards hurrying into camp, copious inventive excuses ready on their lips. But Monck had no taste for delay and told his colonels to stay their hands. Such men would fight the better for a touch of leniency.

As the guns began their bombardment of Dundee, Monck lay down to sleep, wrapped in his cloak, only to be awoken in the dawn as Morgan and Alured clattered triumphantly back into camp.

'Sir! Sir!' the orderly shook his commander-in-chief without ceremony, starting Monck from a dream in which he had lain upon a litter in an improbable suit of golden armour, a coronet upon his head.

'What in God's name …?' The reassuring crump of his guns came to him, as their projectiles landed among the frightened citizens of Dundee, denying them a night's rest and confirming that the garrison had not sallied. Before the orderly could explain, the small figure of Morgan loomed over him.

'Is that you, Tom?' Monck asked, bestirring himself, and wiping he sleep from his eyes. 'How did your matter pass?'

'Well enough, General Monck, if you wish to break your fast with the Earl of Leven, the Earl Marischal and the Earl of Crawford, not to mention three hundred lairds and gentlemen and some heap of church ministers – who are a deal of trouble and certainly not worth your solicitude, let alone your breakfast.'

'You have done well, then.'

'Well, sir? Well? We have bagged the whole lot of them, by God! In my judgment Scotland will be paralysed, but for those savages in the mountains.'

Over breakfast Morgan told his yarn, of how they had reached Alyth unmolested and, to allay suspicion, passed right through the town and bivouacked on its farther side as if an expected reinforcement. After a cool few hours' rest they had reassembled and struck their blow. Entering the town they hurriedly roused it, taking from their beds Alexander Leslie, the Earl of Leven and head of the provisional government King Charles had left in charge of his northern kingdom, along with several other nobles and notables. It was a feat-of-arms worthy of both Morgan and Alured, and Monck said as much.

Later that day, having sent out a second flying column under Okey and Grosvenor, and as the artillery pressed its demands upon the city of Dundee, Monck wrote to Parliament, adopting the formal style beloved by Cromwell, but thinking of the dashing Alured:

It is a very great mercy which the Lord of Hosts hath been pleased to bestow upon us, observing the time and season. This is the Lord's work and therefore he alone ought to have the praise.

That was all very well, he thought, chewing his quill, and should satisfy Alured, but what about Morgan? After a moment he drew up a separate paper and commended the two officers, requesting a colonelcy of dragoons for Morgan. *It is but due recompense for his services here in Scotland*, Monck concluded. He laid down his pen and fell to scratching himself.

'What a damnable country,' he muttered as he sanded and sealed his despatch, calling for William Clarke. 'Have you the rest of the regimental returns for London?' he asked his secretary.

'Everything is ready, sir, and the courier is waiting, and, er …' Clarke held some additional papers.

'There is something else?' queried Monck.

'Yes, General, I have had four reports from different regiments, all of which arise since the regimental returns were made up …'

'Well?'

'There is an outbreak of fever, spotted-fever it is said, among the troops.'

'How many cases?'

Clarke shuffled through the loose sheets. 'Thirty-two, but Grosvenor's surgeon hints at a potential epidemic.'

Monck grunted. 'Send the returns off as they are. I doubt whether London will care much if a few soldiers fall sick.'

He resumed scratching himself as Clarke left the room and then, struck by a thought, unlaced himself to investigate the source of the irritation. 'Dear God!' he muttered, picking the blood-bloated tick from his left flank. 'Spotted-fever!'

The bombardment of Dundee continued, day and night, refusing all summonses to surrender. More guns arrived, along with Hane and his large mortars; serious breaches began to show in the walls as Okey and Grosvenor returned from their sortie. They had penetrated into the Grampian highlands, routing a strong force of Scots horse and taking some one hundred prisoners. Tired and stained, the two colonels stumbled into Monck's headquarters early one morning, the grime on their dust and sweat streaked faces split by broad grins.

'You have done well, gentlemen, very well indeed,' Monck said in a phrase that, unbeknown to him, was passed among the colonels as a mark of high approbation. Monck offered them refreshment, turning aside to scratch himself with a muttered curse. A red rash had appeared upon the backs of his hands.

'How goes the work here?' asked Okey, his mouth full.

'They are stubborn, but we have a breach or two and, since they repudiate my offers of terms, I intend to storm the city tomorrow.'

'Damn fools!' mumbled Okey.

'Aye,' agreed Grosvenor, 'they'll live to regret that.'

'I fear so,' added Monck.

Thus, on the morning of 1 September 1651, Monck began to draw his men up to assault the now very considerable breaches in the city's defences. A further offer of quarter was sent forward and stubbornly rejected, whereupon Monck shrugged; he could do no more out of compassion and gave the order to attack.

The assault would be led by two forlorn hopes, each directed to a separate breach. The western would be stormed by men from Monck's own regiment, led by Captain Hart; the eastern breach would be forced by Colonel Ashfield's regiment and as soon as the defences had been carried, the pioneers under Captain Ely would clear the debris to allow the passage of the horse, three hundred – a dozen from each troop in the army drawn by lot – were to follow the infantry with sword and pistol. A further four hundred seamen had been landed by

Bourne and sent up to reinforce the army, while four hundred horse, all mounted, were to be readied to sweep into the city.

'This,' Monck assured his officers as they assembled for their briefing, 'will enable us to clear the streets faster and with every element of surprise of which we are capable; we shall overwhelm them and the effusion of blood will be thereby lessened.' He paused for their full attention. 'I am keen not to aggravate the citizens the easier to pacify them and reconcile them to our rule but, alas, I must needs give over the city for the customary period of rapine to assuage our men. Do you impress upon your men that this shall last only twenty-four hours. After that, if they get out of hand, I shall administer summary justice, but make plain my intent before the assault. Are there any questions?' He looked round; most stood still, a few shook their heads. 'Very well then. Our word shall be 'God with us' and our sign a white shirt-tail hanging out behind …' A laugh greeted this practical but very necessary precaution. 'Well, as near white as the men can produce and for those of you unable to comply, a white kerchief.'

All was made ready, not least a sprouting of shirt-tails which greatly amused men otherwise sobered by what they were about to undertake. At eleven o'clock the signal was given: a blare of trumpets and impetuous beating of drums. Ominously for those within the defences, the gun fell suddenly silent as, with a self-encouraging roar, the forlorn hopes, east and west, ran at the breaches to be met by a staunch defence. Monck watched from a vantage point; he was not greatly in doubt of his men's success, but he was anxious that their losses would not be great, for many were showing signs of sickness and their numbers were consequently limited, notwithstanding the reinforcements that had come from Nehemiah Bourne's squadron of the fleet.

The forlorn hopes were rapidly reinforced by the onrush of the readied foot and, about twenty minutes after the signal for the assault had been given, Monck was satisfied the defence was crumbling. He mounted his horse and cantered down to join the first line of cavalry as it began to surge forward. As he passed over the mound of dust, stones and debris that, notwithstanding the efforts of Ely's pioneers, made of the breach a small and broken hillock, Monck knew the place was his. The horsemen filled the narrow streets, encouraged by shouts that the enemy was in retreat and holing-up in the church, soon had the church invested and pressed. Groups of the enemy unable to reach this sanctuary were either slain or fell back to the market-square where Monck arrived within a few moments, shouting an order that quarter must be given to those who laid down their arms immediately. For many he was too late; women and children had been ridden down in the narrow streets, the lucky hacked down by the dragoons' swords, the unfortunate trampled under the steel of their horses' shoes. Amid the swirl of attackers and their victims, a party of English soldiers were dragging a richly-dressed man into the square. Monck, recognising the figure of a senior officer, called out for them to hold hard but a fanatic Puritan officer pistolled him as he was brought to his knees at Monck's feet.

'Damn you, sir!' Monck shouted amid the uproar, but the wild light in the Puritan's eyes told that he was beyond the call of human reason.

''Tis Lumsden, the Governor,' another officer said, addressing Monck as he let the bloody corpse fall after turning it over for identification.

Monck looked about him for the officer who had dealt the fatal blow and caught sight of him retreating into the increasing crowd of victorious soldiery that crowded into the market square to the shouts by the defenders of 'Quarter! Quarter!'

'Damn you!' Monck threw the words furiously after the guilty man, who could not possibly have heard him in the uproar. 'Damn you, sir! You have dishonoured me!'

But the death of Lumsden, who had confronted Monck on the bloody field of Dunbar, seemed to have broken all resistance and the cries for quarter now came from all directions. Plunging his horse into the throng Monck raged at his men, sapping their thirst for vengeance, for the fight was over and everywhere the enemy gave way. Seeing the fury in Monck's face most men desisted from their bloody indulgence, fearful that he would have them shot for disobedience and an unnatural calm fell slowly upon the city.

As some five hundred Scots now laid down their weapons in the market-square, Monck received reports that Conyngham was dead. He had, with the garrison of Stirling, marched directly to Dundee to reinforce and warn Lumsden, just as Colonel Okey had predicted.

''Tis a damnable business,' Monck remarked to William Clarke, who rode with him through the streets the following morning, accompanied by an escort of cavalry. Monck observed with distaste the English soldiers at their business of rapine. As the city had failed to surrender when summoned, the laws of war allowed the attacking troops the right of plunder. Monck could not avoid giving it over to this horror, as his men would expect as a reward for their courage in storming the defences, but he had restricted their licence to twenty-four hours.

Turning in his saddle to ask a question of Clarke, he saw the other man's expression. They were passing a tenement from the open windows of which came the screams of women and the roars of drunken soldiery.

Clarke caught Monck's eye. 'God have mercy,' he said, his face pale.

Monck made no response. There was nothing to say. To tell Clarke that this was mild stuff compared with what he had seen on the Continent, would mean little to the other man. Before this war Will Clarke had been a barrister and had not had the schooling of his chief. Besides, how could one compare horrors? Monck turned to their own business, diverting Clarke's mind from what was going on all around him.

'What's the reckoning?' Monck asked.

Clarke took a moment to recover himself, coughed and then responded. 'Along with Lumsden and Conyngham, between four and five hundred soldiers and townspeople are said to have lost their lives, sir.'

''Tis enough. And the cost to our arms?'

'No more than Captain Hart and twenty Englishmen killed,' Clarke reported, his grasp of such details at his command again, 'with a like number wounded.'

''Tis nothing,' Monck murmured to himself.

They had reached the citadel, clattering in under the gate, the sentries pulling themselves to order as they saw the big man on his horse, the flare of a tawny orange sash about his waist and the dozen troopers following in his wake. Here they found Hane happily waving his inventory of captured artillery.

'Well?' said Monck, stilling his mount so that it shook its noble head with a jingle of harness.

'Cannon seized to the number of thirty-eight pieces, General Monck. Besides these we have a fine but currently indeterminate number aboard the scores of ships in the harbour. All are lawful prize.'

Monck nodded silently so that the enthusiastic Hane was uncertain whether his commander-in-chief was pleased as Monck pulled his horse's head round and kicked the rowels of his spurs into its flanks. Turning about the little cavalcade retraced its steps, the horse's hooves striking sparks from the granite flags of the castle courtyard. As they descended into the town and returned to the army's sequestrated headquarters the noise of his men rejoicing at the quantities of plunder engendered a dull and inexplicable rage in Monck. That night he found himself covered by a red rash and tormented by an itch that seemed intractable. This irritation only exacerbated his anger when he learned next day that many of his troops, full of wine and conceit, failed to cease their licensed robbery at the expiry of the term he had allowed them. Bellowing at Clarke, he issued a general order forbidding further looting, along with another compelling the inhabitants to bury the dead. This was not the end of the matter of plunder, but it was the end of Monck's active participation for, on the 5th, he took to his bed, directing operations thereafter through Morgan and his indefatigable secretary, William Clarke.

The attending surgeon confirmed the diagnosis as the tick-borne spotted-fever, which induced diarrhoea and vomiting, manifesting itself by sores and a rash, laying its victim low in a high fever. An infuriated Monck lay sweating on his camp-bed, insisting in his lucid moments that the looting must end and promising visitations of the utmost severity upon any who dared to disobey him, indisposed as he was. And in the moments of feverish delirium he raged incoherently, though Clarke thought he uttered some names with which he, as custodian of the Commander-in-Chief's muster-sheets and Order of Battle, was unfamiliar. Three stood out, as if of especial importance to the restless Monck, but who 'Battyn' and 'Ratsford' were, Clarke had no idea, though he knew the identity of 'Anne'.

Amid the wilder onsets of his fever, the General lay quiet, his mind recovering its great responsibilities and articulating his policy. 'This shall be no Drogheda,' he told Clarke, referring to Cromwell's eternal shame, and signing the death-warrants brought to him as his colonels carried out the court-martials on those English soldiers foolish enough to disregard the General's order. 'I have no wish to harry the Scots, nor to press then beyond their means,' he told Clarke. 'All are subject to the law, the military more than most for the military must be governed with a severity matching that licence allowed them by the profession of arms. We must be kind to the Scots, Will, and I have been dishonoured enough,' he complained, as Clarke took the quill from him and he sank back into his pillows, sodden with perspiration.

*

For several days Monck lay prostrated by his illness, attended by a Scots physician, James Macrae, whom Clarke had found for him in the city. Fortunately Thomas Morgan knew his strategy and William Clarke his mind. In this wise the two men faithfully pressed matters forward and, on 11 September, William Clarke wrote to Mr Speaker Lenthall informing Parliament that:

It hath pleased Almighty God to visit Lieutenant General Monck with a very desperate sickness since the taking of this town, but we hope he is in a very good way of recovery. He is a very precious instrument, and the most perfectly fitted for management of affairs here. His temper every way fits him for this employment, and none could order the Scots so handsomely as himself, he carries things with such a grace and rigid gentleness …

Unaware of this eulogium, or of the effect his firm hand had upon those now subject to his authority, Monck sweated the days away, his brighter hours occupied by confirming those orders issued under his name by Morgan. Alerted by information garnered by Clarke's Intelligence Department, Morgan dispatched a series of flying columns to supress any resistance encouraged by the 'news' from England that King Charles had flung aside all resistance and was even then in London.

But the falsity of this rumour was soon known, for the incontrovertible facts inevitably reached Dundee. On 3rd September; exactly a year after Dunbar to the very day, that of Cromwell's birthday, Charles and his Scots Army had been utterly defeated at Worcester by the pursuing English. It was averred that the Royalist army had been scattered to the four winds and the countryside was being scoured for fugitives, including Charles himself. And while there were those who did not at first believe it, it was soon put beyond doubt; the only ray of hope that sustained the Royalists was the consideration that Charles himself had escaped with his life and was thus sent upon his travels once again.

*

It was mid-October before Monck rose unsteadily from his sickbed to query Clarke as to how many ships had arrived at Leith with supplies for his army and to pick up the details of his administration. And it was the end of the month before he could sit his horse sufficiently steadily to inspect his troops. Although in the meanwhile Morgan and his colleagues had reduced the remaining pockets of resistance in the Highlands and, on Monck's orders, sent troops across the Pentland Firth to garrison the Orkneys, there was trouble in the ranks. This was being led by Colonel Alured and it was news of this which, despite their unwillingness to overburden a man recently at death's door, both Morgan and Clarke were agreed, could not be concealed from the General.

Both men had therefore urged Monck to show himself at a review of those troops quartered in the environs of the Scots city and to take advantage of Alured's presence by confronting him with his disloyal dissension. Dressed in half-armour, his left arm bent and its gloved hand set upon the enormous silk knot of his extravagant red-gold sash, his right lightly holding the reins of his favourite charger, Monck rode along the ranks, his keen eye raking the men's faces and catching their eyes. He hoped they knew how much he laboured in their interest for most of his anxieties were concerned with their well-being. It was a beautiful, cloudless morning and the sun had burnt off an early frost. The spectacle had drawn a crowd of the citizenry who stood watching this show of military force. At Monck's side, his horse's head half a length behind the General, rode Colonel Thomas Morgan, and behind came half a dozen others, including Will Clarke.

From time-to-time Monck would pause, sometimes in front of a common soldier, or a trooper whom he would affect to recognise and enquire if the man's billet or cantonment as well as his victuals were to his satisfaction. Occasionally he would ask a match-lock to be presented and enquire how many live charges the arquebusier drew for service. Invariably he drew rein alongside each regimental commander, returning the officer's salute with a casual nod of his own beplumed and wide-brimmed hat.

As the little cavalcade approached the troopers of Alured's cavalry, their Colonel at their head, Monck said without turning, 'I shall summon Alured to confer after this work is done, Tom. Do you linger awhile and press him to bring his cronies with him. Now drop back a touch.'

'Very well, sir,' Morgan acknowledged, slowing his horse. Behind him the staff did likewise.

A moment later Monck, closing his knees tight about his saddle, tugged at his reins and brought his charger's head back with such a jerk that the stallion reared, flecked foam from its mouth and, its front hooves momentarily pawing the air, caused Alured's horse to start.

Alured was taken by surprise, as Monck intended, but kept his seat as Monck did his.

'There, there,' said Monck patting his horse's neck as it recovered itself and stood, hard-reined and snorting, in front of Alured. 'I give you God's good day, Colonel,' Monck smiled at the discomfited cavalryman who was struggling to regain his composure as he mastered his own nervous mount.

'God day, General,' muttered Alured.

'Your men look well, sir, I trust there are no shortcomings among them?'

'They are as well as can be expected, sir.'

'Oh? That does not sound very satisfactory. Pray, do you take wine with me after this is done with. Until then, sir, I wish you well.' Monck eased his rein and kicked his mount into motion. Out of the corner of his eye, as he turned his head to run his eyes over the front rank of Alured's senior troop, he saw Morgan slide alongside Alured and whisper in his ear.

An hour later Monck received Alured and his party in his quarters in the castle. He was alone but for Morgan and Clarke. Morgan was seated and held a glass of wine while Clarke stood at the General's table quietly discussing some papers. Monck did not look up when the orderly announced the new arrivals, but he raised his eyes sufficiently to count the boots of perhaps ten or a dozen men, Morgan had done his work well. With luck Alured had taken the bait and, galled by Monck's attempt to make him look a fool in front of his men, had been angry enough to muster all those of like mind to himself.

Monck waited until the boots began shuffling, then he looked up. 'You have a lot of friends, it seems, Colonel Alured. Give them some wine, Will, if we have sufficient glasses.' There was a moment or two of further shuffling during which Monck nodded to Morgan, who rose and walked to the door through which the gathering had just arrived and, passing through, closed it behind him. As the group settled Monck fixed Alured with a cold and disenchanting glare.

'This,' Monck nodded at the assembly, 'has the appearance of a deputation, Colonel, and if this is the case I suggest you disburden yourself of your grievances. Colonel Morgan has a guard without and I would not have you leave this chamber without knowing your mind.'

Alured flushed and hesitated; those about him coughed awkwardly. Then, as Monck held out a hand for a document Clarke had been schooled to have ready just as Alured opened his mouth to speak, someone at the rear began a catalogue of complaints.

'Aye, we have grievances by the score, General. We who do the Lord's work, who labour even on the Sabbath to accomplish what God wills against the faithless heathen …'

'Silence, sir!' Monck roared. 'I will not have the officers of the New Model rant at me like crossroads preachers. I asked Colonel Alured what particulars he held as disputatious …' Silence had fallen on the room. 'Now, sir, what is it that so troubles you?'

Alured lowered his head, unable to meet Monck's furious glare. 'It was the affair at Alyth, General Monck …' Alured's opening words were met by a low murmur of agreement. 'Most of those here were of the party that took the place…'

'I know that!' snapped Monck.

'Then you should also know that I … er, we … feel our services to have been, er, unrewarded.'

Monck shoved the paper he was holding under Alured's nose. 'There! Read that! As for the rest of you I am appalled that officers of the New Model should whine and cavil like common soldiers grumbling over their cooking pots. What measures do you take when your men complain? Why you rectify those you can and pass those you cannot to others of superior rank, but what think you of a soldier who does his duty them complains he *has not had sufficient recompense*?' This last Monck uttered with the utmost contempt. 'You have your pay which follows the taking of your oath – more than you have had on previous service. You are officers and officers are bound to exert themselves, why else should they exist? A soldier labours for his pay, and officer serves for his honour.' He paused a moment to let this particular point sink in before continuing. 'As for your religious beliefs they are for you to compose with God Almighty. They shall not – shall *never* – obtrude in between thy service to the State, for they are at once the same thing.' They were deadly quiet now and few met his gaze as he looked from one to the other.

'Gentlemen,' he changed his tone, making it conciliatory, 'you are they who snatched victory from defeat on the field of Dunbar. Do not dishonour that achievement because the consequences of that victory wear you out. We are set to bring the Scots to a betterment of their lot. *That* is God's work ... Now, to your duties.' He raised his voice: 'Colonel Morgan!'

The door of the chamber opened and the chastened officers filed out. Only Morgan and the two regular sentinels stood in the antechamber; there was no other guard. As for Alured, he had read the copy of Monck's letter of commendation to London and now handed it back to Monck.

'I did my best for you, Colonel,' Monck said, taking it.

Unable to say anything Alured dropped his eyes, stepped backwards, drew himself up and executed a short bow to Monck. 'Sir,' he managed before turning and leaving the room.

In the weeks and months that followed Monck consolidated his government over most of Scotland. The Highlands had been effectively isolated and although pockets of resistance existed in the west, particularly in the Isle of Arran, his judicious measures in civil government, backed by his detached sense of fairness and his lack of triumphalism, won him among the Scots nobility and gentry – if not friends - then reluctant admirers. While that greatest of Scottish noblemen Archibald Campbell, the Earl of Argyll, remained aloof, his namesake John Campbell, a former Lord Chancellor of Scotland and Earl of Loudon, Alexander Lindsay, the Lord Balcarres and a Covenanter, together with that eminent Roman Catholic and head of the powerful Gordons, the Marquess of Huntly, all submitted on Monck's promise of protection if they did nothing prejudicial to the Commonwealth. By degrees, their defeat seemed less bitter to them.

By January 1652, despite the persistent pain in his legs, Monck was fit enough to meet John Lambert, his old colleague Richard Deane and the dozen other English Commissioners sent from London to carry out negotiations with the Scottish delegates. Most of these men were sympathetic to the plight of the Scots and, under Monck's influence, they reduced the punitive tax Parliament wished to levy upon them too indemnify the English for the cost of the campaign. Thereafter both Monck and Lambert toiled together for several weeks in what passed for amity in the face of the Scots delegation, successfully bringing the parties together sufficiently to proclaim the twenty-one Scottish deputies to be sent south to negotiate the terms of a Union between England and Scotland. Many Scots considered this Union to be little better than the condition of a blackbird eaten by a hawk, but as trade picked up and prospered, many Scots – particularly the mercantile classes in the larger towns – became reconciled to the turn events had taken and Monck's government was seen by some as less rapacious that that which had preceded it.

*

'Well sir,' Lambert said, his face a mask of polite formality as he climbed into the coach alongside Monck, nodding at William Clarke sitting opposite and clutching Monck's voluminous leather despatch bag, 'I am sorry for your indisposition and hope it does not long compromise you.'

'That is kind of you,' Monck replied with equal politesse as he made way for the younger man.

'I am of a mind to reach London without delay,' Lambert added, revealing the true reason for his concern.

Despite the pain in his legs to which he had, perforce, to reconcile himself, Monck smiled, penetrating Lambert's smoke-screen. It was a month later and their task on conciliation between the Scots and the occupying English was over. Monck was relieved of his command in the face of his ill-health and had handed over his governorship to Richard Deane. Now he and Lambert shared a carriage and escort on the road south.

'You will be eager to reach Dublin, no doubt,' Monck remarked, referring to Lambert's new appointment.

'When the public service calls, General Monck, a man must answer it with some despatch,' Lambert remarked sententiously.

Monck grunted, recalling Lambert, like Clarke, was a lawyer. 'Indeed, General Lambert, indeed,' he agreed drily.

They parted company at Berwick after a night's lodging there, Monck pleading the pain in his legs required a slower pace than that upon which Lambert insisted. The younger man agreed to leave the conveyance to the invalid. Clambering onto the horse he had ordered be made ready, Lambert looked down at Monck as he stood beside the open door of the carriage to bid him farewell. 'I give you God's love, General Monck.'

'God go with you, General Lambert.'

Monck watched Lambert and his escort of Ironsides clatter away down the London road. 'There goes ambition,' he thought to himself, staring after the younger man with a tinge of envy. He had nothing to reproach himself for; his tenure of the chief command in Scotland had been the nearest thing to a triumph that the head of a victorious army of occupation could achieve. Even now Deane had begun the last phase of the pacification of Scotland in the English interest, but Monck nevertheless nursed a sense of grievance that his fever and its after-effects had deprived him of that final triumph. Not only was his sense of self-worth cheated, his disease had robbed him of some private wealth. It was, he felt, a high price to pay, in all senses of the phrase, for the door of opportunity was, he felt, now closing in his face.

Before leaving Edinburgh he had written to Anne, telling her that he was coming south and hoped to be with her before the end of the month. She had had a long wait, a wait that must have tried her sorely, for she had written to him herself, her short, painfully contrived missives reaching him by way of the Army despatches.

Now, as Lambert and his troop of cavalry rode off, Monck looked about him, breathing in the sharp morning air before submitting to the stuffy confinement of the coach. He stared back along the road to where it crossed the River Tweed which sparkled in the early morning sunshine, unconsciously rubbing his aching legs. He could not then know that the pain would trouble him for the rest of his life, nor that he too would one day cross the Tweed on an occasion infinitely more momentous than Lambert's hurried progress or his own slow retirement. At that moment it seemed that he had done all a man might reasonably be expected to do in the service of the Commonwealth.

Turning to the open door of the coach he nodded to the cornet commanding his now reduced escort, clambered in and subsided with a groan upon the padded seat. He nodded at William Clarke who had, in accordance with the etiquette, entered the coach some moments earlier and had been patiently awaiting his chief. A minute later the equipage lurched forward as the horses' hooves struck the stones and they took up their burden.

'Think you we left Scotland in a better state than we found it, Will?'

'I have no doubt of it, sir.'

'But they did not invite us to improve them,' Monck responded.

'No, sir, they did not. But some things are best left to God.'

Monck smiled and looked at Clarke. 'Do you truly think that all that happens is God's will?'

'Well … I, er …'

'Or does man purpose what his ambition drives him to and is it God's function to act as moderator?' Monck paused as Clarke considered this proposition. But any response he was considering was cut short by Monck. 'Come Will, thy wits must need work and argument for both principles if thou art to resume thy duties pleading contrary cases in court.'

'I have not thought of returning to the law, General. I am for Dundee once your own affairs are settled.'

'Ah, yes, I had forgot. And you shall take your wife back with you?'

Clarke nodded. 'Yes, Dorothy expects to join me now matters are better settled.'

'Then I wish you both well.'

'And you, sir?' Clarke asked, aware that Monck had a paramour hidden away in the West Country.

Monck blew out his cheeks. 'Well, once we have drawn our present business to a conclusion in London,' he said, nodding to the despatch case behind Clarke's legs which contained the documents to be laid before Parliament as justification for Monck's governorship, 'then I think I must try Bath and discover what relief the waters might provide for my distemper.' He paused, then went on, 'I shall not be called upon to serve again for my health is too broken down.'

After a few moments of silence as Clarke digested he said, 'Should you change your mind, sir, or should you be summonsed to take upon yourself further duties for the common weal I beg that you recall me to your service, sir.'

Monck studied his colleague for a long time and then nodded. 'Very well, though it is unlikely enough. But you have been indispensable Will, and I am indebted to you.'

'It has not been a hardship, sir, to serve under you,' Clarke said.

'I am truly touched, Will, and I thank you for it.'

An easy and companionable silence grew between them as each became lost in his own private thoughts. The curtailment of his Governorship of Scotland may have deprived Monck of full recompense but there was no denying Parliament had voted him a handsome sum of money for his services. There was some consolation in that, to be sure, and although he was in for a damned tedious journey, at least at the end of it he would see Anne. Bath, he thought, would provide a cure for his sorry carcass if any cure was to be had, and then they could lose themselves in the green loveliness of the Torridge valley, marry and enjoy a quiet life. Once he had …

He looked at Clarke. The man had fallen asleep, his head lolling as the carriage jolted its uncomfortable way south. Clarke was clever, his barrister's sharp mind had made him a smart collector and sifter of intelligence and he had embraced

Monck's methods as if they had been his own. Indeed, as the head of Monck's Intelligence Department he had had access to all manner of secret information, some of which lay in the satchel tucked behind his legs. For perhaps half an hour Monck considered seeking Clarke's advice on the question for which he had assured Anne he had found an answer. The problem was that the answer required him to hazard his honour as much as his honesty and while he had been minded to gamble upon that two years ago, he was less certain now. Of a sudden he resolved not to involve Clarke. Such a man might be helpful, but Monck had no further appetite for selling his soul as a hostage to fortune. He knew himself not to be one of fortune's favourites like John Lambert. Some men fell naturally into the way of advantage and saw their good luck as a reward for virtue. Lambert was one such and Oliver might have been another except that Monck divined him to be a man of honest humility, a true God-fearing man.

Monck shuddered at the train of thought thus initiated, looking up sharply to see whether the sudden movement had disturbed Clarke, but the younger man remained asleep. Why was he so troubled about his own honour? And how come Cromwell obtruded, as if dragged from the recesses of his own, inner self to somehow reproach him. The thought puzzled him so that he frowned, his weather-beaten brow furrowing with the effort of thought as he disinterred the object of his mental quest with an audible gasp of horror.

It was Oliver, of course; Oliver who had taken his all-or-nothing advice over defeating the Irish and had in consequence laid waste to Drogheda, burning those who had taken refuge in its church. The horror of it had penetrated Monck's fevered unconsciousness even as he had languished on his sickbed in Edinburgh, the high fever augmenting its hellish terrors. That one might plead military necessity was one thing, but Oliver boasted of it before Parliament as if it were a redemptive act. Monck had never advised that. He slumped back into the hard cushions, a sheen of sweat on his features: it was all too late now. Dunbar had supervened, the business of Scotland had occupied him and so it was not until now, in the hours of enforced idleness when he had to answer for his own conduct before the Bar of the Commons that Monck had taken stock. Why had Cromwell, a man destiny had placed in high and influential office, failed to grasp the precise tenets of his profession as Monck had done? Why had he not tempered his conduct in the way that Monck had himself outlined in his *Observations* on war, for such must be obvious to a man as intelligent as Oliver? Had Monck overplayed his hand when he advised Cromwell at Milford? Perhaps.

'Too little of the fox,' Monck murmured to himself.

'Wh-what is that you say, sir?' Opposite Clarke started awake.

'Eh? Oh, nothing, I must have been talking to myself.'

Clarke's intervention brought Monck out of his gloomy introspection but reminded him of something else, something quite different unless it was a similarity of misfortune. 'I was just thinking that while in London I should wait upon Bishop Wren ...'

'You would return to The Tower?' Clarke was puzzled.

'Aye. The man has been there too long and must want some amusement.'

'He will stay there yet some time,' Clarke added.

Monck nodded. 'Yes, that is quite probably the case.'

But the contemplation of executing a good work had soothed Monck's troubled mind a little so that, as the coach lurched and bumped along, he too fell into a fitful doze. The Tower reminded him of Anne and their early meetings. Oliver must make his own composition with God. God would know the difference between the intentions of the two men. George Monck would visit Wren and, in passing through London – and all alone – he would lay the ghost of Ratsford.

Read on for the first chapter of *The Tempering*: Book Two in the *Sword of State* series

SWORD OF STATE
THE TEMPERING

LONDON
March 1652

Monck pushed the empty platter away from him and took another swig at the tankard of small beer provided by his landlady. It tasted sour in his mouth, adding to the black mood which had dogged him all day and was exacerbated by the rattling shutters which told that outside March was going out like a lion – and a wet one at that. He was angry with himself – furious, in fact – aware that he had drunk excessively last night when dining with Lord Conway. Ned Conway had served with him in Ulster and Monck's enjoyment of his old colleague's company had led him to say too much about himself. Now, twenty-four hours later, he chid himself: it was true that he was bored by apparently useless weeks of waiting in London, but that was no excuse for a loose tongue. Always a guarded man, Monck had let slip his caution in the conviviality of the meeting by revealing his intention to abandon his military career and then marry. His only consolation was that Conway went to bed a good deal drunker than Monck himself, for the General had a prodigious capacity for wine, one of the many features of his remarkable character that impressed itself upon his subordinate officers. Moreover, Monck thought, raking over what he could recall of the detail of their conversation, Conway had gone to his bed with the impression that Monck's intended was the widow of Ned's uncle, Edward Popham. If that was the case, he had perhaps not compromised himself as much as he thought, though the lady concerned might not think so, should she hear of the impropriety. Well, the milk was spilt now but, had his idle presence in London not hinged on the question of matrimony, Monck would have long ago joined Anne in the old manor-house at Potheridge on the banks of the Torridge in Devon where she patiently awaited his long-delayed return. She had expected him there after he had taken the waters at Bath, seeking a cure for his bad legs but he had instead returned directly to London, unwilling to put her in danger until this whole damnable matter was cleared-up; after all, adultery was a hanging offence and Monck had earned a deep respect for the rule of law.

He emptied the ale-pot, leaned back in his chair and regarded the room in which he was quartered with a jaundiced eye. After his long service in Scotland, ended by a near-fatal attack of the spotted-fever that had apparently wrecked his health, he had hoped to go home to Anne and Potheridge. Instead he was stuck here, in cheap lodgings in Westminster. The twin candles on the small table at which he sat guttered as the gale outside penetrated the room and set the shadows about him dancing on the grubby walls. He had endured far worse quarters during his long years of campaigning, to be sure, often sleeping in the open, wrapped in his cloak.

'Dunbar,' he murmured to himself. He had slept in his sodden cloak that night, by Heaven! He recalled the eve of the battle outside the Scottish sea-port with a wry smile, remembering with a quickening of the pulse – for their plight had come perilously close to utter catastrophe – how the English Army's line of retreat had been cut off by Leslie's out-numbering Scots. And how Cromwell had chewed his lower lip until it bled! But the Lord General had given John Lambert most of the credit for the victory that had so remarkably turned the tables on Leslie and so dramatically reversed the fortunes of the English Army in Scotland. Not that Cromwell had kept his own achievement out of his despatch, but the young and charming Lambert had been selected for especial praise. Monck's own part in changing the Army's fate had been set aside, though Oliver had left him Governor of the northern Nation while he raced off in hot pursuit of Charles Stuart and crushed him at Worcester exactly a year later.

Was that only six months ago? It seemed almost half a lifetime to Monck as he recalled the subsequent agonies of the spotted-fever to which he had succumbed after pacifying most of Scotland. It was not just his legs that had suffered from the disease; it seemed his mind had been affected. His physician, an Edinburgh man engaged by his military secretary, the faithful William Clarke, had seemed to take some delight in explaining to the English commander, that 'his fever o'erheated his brain which, simmering within the skull might, might, mind ye, have a permanent effect upon Your Excellency's mental faculties'.

'In what way?' Monck had gasped, his eyes swimming in their burning sockets.

Macrae had shrugged his shoulders. 'I canna tell, sir, but it might reduce one's deductive powers. There is nae telling.' The quack had paused, relishing his small triumph over his country's conqueror. 'Or it could put ye oot of sorts, induce a moodiness foreign to your nature heretofore. But one canna be certain o' sich matters and only time will tell and time might – *might*, mind ye – prove a better healer.'

'I *am* reassured,' Monck had murmured sarcastically from his damp pillow.

'Broth, sir, guid beef broth, is your best specific.'

Monck had nodded weakly and closed his eyes. Now he thought the lugubrious Scot correct. Here was a moodiness settled upon him that was certainly foreign to him 'heretofore'. He sighed, then another thought struck him. It was all nonsense; at the root of his black mood was the ancient shadow of a dead man, Nicholas Battyn, whose maledictions followed Monck like a gypsy's curse. Always some sadness triggered the damnable memory of Battyn and the extreme folly of Monck's youthful and intemperate outburst. He had narrowly escaped the gallows for his misconduct and felt the beating of Battyn to be his personal, consequential and spiritually fatal original sin. Its memory burned him even at this remove of time, assailing him at low moments, bringing its evil as explanation of every unfortunate circumstance that subsequently impinged upon him; it was as if – illogically, but convincingly – his very being turned upon it. Indeed, he could even persuade himself that King Charles's failure to take his advice and recruit and train a small effective army before his enemies did just that, rested entirely upon the adolescent misdemeanour of his advisor – George Monck. Had not the

King himself raised the matter of Monck's intemperance when they had walked together in Christchurch garden? It was as though he, George Monck, had begun a chain of events that had led Charles to the scaffold and that the very thing Monck sought more than anything, peace for his country, had in fact been placed entirely beyond accomplishment by his own stupidity! Men who quailed before the severity of the terrible General Monck's glare could not imagine the tough old soldier's thoughts running through the dark pursued by such a demon! And oh, how he longed for that peace, both for himself and for his country.

He stirred himself; Macrae had been right: his brain was fried, frizzled and useless. There were men abroad whose sins far eclipsed those of George Monck. Had the King's cause – or any cause, for that matter – been fatally affected by *their* peccant actions? Or was the world's mess a product of it all? A grand combination? He almost laughed to himself. That, at least, was a certainty!

He had said something of the sort to Bishop Wren two days earlier when, unable to do anything other than await the result of the enquiries he had put in train, Monck had visited the poor man who still lay a prisoner in The Tower. He flattered himself that Wren had been pleased to see his former fellow-prisoner, for he expressed concern that Monck dared show himself there.

'You will compromise yourself, General, talking to a confirmed Royalist and like to languish until I die for it.'

'Well, my Lord Bishop, I do not come under any pretence of trying to persuade you to recant and renounce your loyalties…'

'As *you* have done,' Wren had snapped, pointedly, and Monck saw the wearying excoriation that had borne down upon the prisoner during his long imprisonment. He had turned the rebuke aside as gently as was in his power. Wren had been kind to him when he had occupied an adjacent cell and Monck was not a man to forget a kindness.

'Come, my Lord Bishop, you well know from our lengthy discussions in this place that I place duty to my country above everything.'

''Twas some time past,' Wren had riposted.

'Aye, and time has worked its worst upon us both. Thou art testy and I am distempered…'

'You are sick?'

'Compromised. I am not minded to serve again.'

He had gone on to tell Wren of the trials he had suffered thanks to the spotted-fever. He made no appeal for sympathy; that was not to be expected of the old soldier. He simply explained the state of his health. The confession of physical weakness had roused Wren's concern, not just for Monck, but for himself.

'I am sorry to hear of such a disabling infirmity,' Wren had said. 'Thou art the only man of standing who might help me in mine own situation.' He gestured at his surroundings. 'You smile…'

'Aye, I should not and I do not mock thee, but it is more comfortable that half the camps and bivouacs I have enjoyed since first I went out from this place.'

'Ah, and when you went the wench went with you. It took some time for us to find another washer-woman half as diligent.'

'That is because Anne was something more than a common washer-woman,' Monck said quickly.

Wren was unmoved by this and went on: 'Do you wish to make your confession, for I hear that you have shamelessly broken the Seventh Commandment with her?'

Monck laughed. 'There are those who would cheerfully see me hang for it, my Lord Bishop, but 'tis a minor peccadillo and I purpose to marry her.'

'I suppose I could grant you absolution on such a promise if 'twere on oath.'

Monck rose and Wren recognised again the physical presence of the man. He went to the door and shouted for the turn-key before addressing Wren. 'You know my opinion of oaths,' he said, and a moment later Wren was alone again in his cell.

Thinking of the visit Monk rather regretted he had made it. He had presumed rather too familiarly upon their former friendship. Two or so years had not been kind to Wren and he was probably right; in all likelihood he would indeed die in The Tower.

Monck set the recollection aside, rubbing his calves as the dull ache reminded him of his own tribulations. The one element of luck that had thus far attended his career, his lack of wounds in battle, seemed set at nought by the perversity of chronic ailment. But what annoyed him most, and sounded too peevish to communicate even to Wren, was that the spotted-fever had robbed him of his own laurels. True, Parliament had voted him a substantial grant, but it was nothing compared to that lavished on Oliver's darling, John Lambert.

Perhaps such a loss of perquisites entitled a man used to such disappointments to soak himself in wine just-the-once, he thought, turning again to his encounter with Ned Conway. And perhaps, despite his misgivings, he might not have let too much slip to Conway. Anyhow, God knew he was utterly fed-up with this fruitless, idle, good-for-nothing waiting – and for what? No news. No news at all. He should be gone, he thought with a sudden resolution, into the West Country where Anne, bless her lonely but constant heart, was waiting for him. Or off into Ireland where he must needs see what disorder had been wrought in the land-grants Parliament had reluctantly given him for an earlier campaign than that in Scotland. Anywhere was better that London. What he had set in train in London was simply not working, for he would have heard something long since.

There was the other matter, too. He must put-up his sword. It was time for George Monck the soldier to overcome the wretched and inadequate motions of George Monck the lover. He dismissed the rumours of increasing difficulties with the Dutch which were most likely to lead to war; to the Devil with that! George Monck had other fish to fry. His admission to Conway that he intended to marry was quite true, whomsoever

Ned thought of as Monck's intended, but it was Anne to whom he had plighted his troth months ago with a handfasting, and it was with Anne that he had been living as openly as they dared in a land where adultery risked the gallows. There, that was the rub; Anne had – or had had – a husband. And the question of which of these alternatives prevailed was the reason why Monck languished so uncharacteristically supine in a Westminster tavern. No-one knew whether the brutal Ratsford – who had abandoned Anne some four years earlier after robbing her of her life's savings – was alive or dead. All his enquiries had come to nothing.

In a characteristically decisive move Monck rose, went to the door and called out for the maid. When the girl came he ordered the table cleared and her mistress sent for. When Mistress Franks appeared, puffing from the tap-room, obsequious and as eager-to-please as any woman should be who quartered a General Officer in the Commonwealth Army under her roof, he ordered her to compound his account.

'I intend leaving tomorrow,' he said, 'and thank you for your many kindnesses to me.'

'It is always a pleasure, sir, to have so distinguished a personage lodging in my house,' she said bobbing away.

Monck smiled at her. 'Come Mistress Franks,' he said in his most winning tone of voice with its soft, attractive West-Country burr, 'but you sound like one of the Members of the Parliament House who frequent your premises all-too-often.'

'Thank you, sir,' she said, making Monck grin the more. 'I hope the weather improves; 'tis no season to be travelling sir.'

He bit off the riposte that he was a soldier and was not used to the luxury of choosing when he should march, temporising that it might moderate by the morning.

'Perhaps,' she said, withdrawing.

Monck turned from the closed door and began to gather up his papers and books, stuffing them into the battered portmanteau that stood at the foot of the bed. The shutters rattled again with an ominous intensity, and he heard the howl of the gale. At least he did not have to venture out tonight, he thought to himself, as he completed packing his most personal effects. Ten minutes later he blew out the candles and betook himself to bed.

No more than twenty-minutes had passed before he heard his name called; the tone was insistent. Mistress Franks stood in the open doorway with a rush dip and Monck sensed something amiss.

'What is it? Is there a fire?'

'No, sir, but a man who insists upon my disturbing you.'

'Does he by God!' Monck stared at the woman a moment, then realised this was no tomfoolery. 'Very well. Give me a moment, then send him in… Wait, do you light my candles, I have packed my tinder-box.' Waiting until she had done his bidding, Monck threw off the bedding and grabbed his robe. A moment later a sodden, thin visaged man stood dripping before him as Mistress Franks waited curiously.

For a moment Monck did not recognise him and had to be prompted as the man took off his hat, its brim spilling its contents on the floor-boards. 'Wragg, General Monck, Mr Humphrey's confidential clerk…'

'Mistress Franks, a glass of toddy for this poor fellow. Come, sit down Mr Wragg… Surely some alarum must have occurred that you must…' Monck broke off, staring at the shivering clerk.

'Mr Humphrey argued, sir,' Wragg began, 'that as I could reach you before midnight and that you had yourself insisted most emphatically, sir, most emphatically if I might say so sir, that the moment we learned anything about, er, about the personal and confidential matter you had honoured us and entrusted us with, then you required immediate notice. Immediate notice, sir. Hence, sir, my reason for disturbing you…' here the loquacious Wragg gestured towards Monck's dishabille, 'at this hour. I trust this is congruent with your wishes.'

'If you have brought me some intelligence, Mr Wragg, then it is most congruent,' Monck responded eagerly, watching as the clerk leant down and began to undo the wet leather satchel he had placed on the floor beside his chair. At this point

Mistress Franks reappeared with two glasses of steaming rum-toddy.

'I did not mean…' Monck began as she handed one to him, but shook his head and smiled. 'No matter…' He could visualise the augmentation of his account thanks to the unannounced visit of Mr Wragg. He only hoped that the news the soaking messenger brought him was what he had so longed for. It might be quite otherwise, as this late intrusion suggested.

'Thank you Mr Wragg.' Monck took the missive from Wragg's outstretched hand. While Wragg fell to the consumption of his pint of toddy, Monck gingerly broke the seal, angled the letter towards the candles and began to read, ignoring Humphrey's pompous superscription for which, it crossed his mind, he would also doubtless pay heavily.

Sir,

I am pleased to inform you that, after extensive and assiduous enquiries pursued with the utmost and most industrious diligence, we have at last secured both intelligence of the party for whom you previously enquired but, by further a pursuit of your Excellency's objective, have to hand this very evening an affidavit to the effect that the man Ratsford succumbed to a visitation of the plague in Smyrna some thirteen months since…

Monck read no further, but looked up sharply at Wragg. 'You have the affidavit?' he enquired shortly, his tone expectant.

Wragg shook his head. 'No, sir. In view of the lateness of the hour, the danger of footpads, the inclemency of the weather…'

'Damn it!' Monck swore, tearing off his robe and hurriedly ridding himself of his night-shirt as a startled Wragg looked-on. Reaching for his shirt and breeches Monck rapped out his intentions. 'Do you wait for me below. I'll be down directly…'

'But General, Mr Humphrey has given me permission, in view of the inclemency of the weather and the lateness of the hour, to remain here the night…'

Monck was already drawing on his heavy boots. 'That is as you wish, Mr Wragg, and as I shall be paying for your accommodation you may avail yourself of my bed but I must tell you that I am to your master without delay.'

'Then I must needs come with you, sir, for you cannot intrude alone…' The wretched Wragg fell to a muttering of 'oh, dear, oh dear,' between rapid quaffings of the stiff toddy Mistress Franks had supplied. Monck polished his own off as he drew on coat and cloak. That done, and as if an after-thought, he turned to his open portmanteau and drew out a soft leather purse, stuffing it into his breast. Then, gathering up his hat, Monck turned to the clerk.

'Come sir, the sooner we go, the sooner we arrive.'

The gale met them at the inn doorway and nearly carried away Monck's wide-brimmed hat. Behind him Wragg quailed visibly at the prospect of the walk to the City where, near the Temple church, Humphreys kept his rooms.

'At least it has stopped raining, Mr Wragg,' Monck said with an encouraging air of joviality. Was this news that Wragg had brought really true? *Could* it be true?

Expectation kept Monck trudging determinedly through streets mired by the torrential rain with the wretched Wragg trailing behind him, all the while uttering imprecations under his breath. They slithered eastwards, passing the watch as midnight was called and were suffered to proceed unmolested, for it was clear by his bearing that Monck was a man of consequence that would brook no half-hearted arrest. As for footpads, the gentlemen of the night had sensibly taken themselves to their beds, whether such a place was a cold nook or a warm midden-heap. Monck sensed Wragg's apprehension grew with the increasing proximity to his master's door.

By the time they arrived the sky had cleared, the thick overcast vanishing with a shift of the wind. Overhead, where the sky could be seen between the over-hanging houses, the stars shone crystal-bright, though rain still tinkled in the gutters and drain-pipes and ran across the slime and mire of the street. The change in the weather matched Monck's mood and he was insensible to Humphrey's protestations of outrage at having so unceremoniously been summoned from his bed. These, in any case, vanished when he realised for whom he had been woken.

'General Monck...' he began with an obsequiousness that far out-matched Mistress Franks's servility, prompting Monck to wonder what sum Humphrey was amassing at his own expense.

'I understand you have an affidavit for me, Mr Humphrey.'

'Yes, yes. Come in sir, come in. Mr Wragg do you...'

'Do you find it Mr Humphrey,' Monck broke in. 'Mr Wragg has done all in his power this night and the poor man will be beyond serving you if he wants another minute to his bed-time.' Monck's tone was peremptory and he turned to Wragg. 'Be off with you sir. I shall not forget your service this evening.'

Thus so uncertainly dismissed, Wragg withdrew and vanished into the darkness.

'Of course...of course...' said Humphrey waving Monck inside and leading him to his office where he transferred the flame from his bedside taper to a muster of half-consumed candles standing upon his desk. Taking a key from about his neck, the lawyer unlocked a drawer and lifted a paper from the pile that lay within, handing it to the General.

'There sir. That should satisfy thee.'

Monck took the paper with a grunt and read:

I, Jacob Harbottle, lately Mate of the good ship Peter of Harwich do most solemnly swear that of my certain knowledge one Ratsford, rated landsman aboard the said ship Peter *of Harwich is deceased in this wise: that he did contract a fever at the Turkic port of Smyrna, from which he took a fatal contagion and expired soon thereafter. This occurring, as best my memory serves, at or near the beginning of February last.*

'Over a year ago,' Monck said, looking up at Humphrey.

'Indeed, General.'

'And how did you locate this man Harbottle?'

'Through an extensive enquiry in every ale-house, whore-house, stew, rookery, nook, cranny and crevice all along the Ratcliffe Highway from The Tower to Limehouse and beyond,' Humphrey said before succumbing to an eloquent yawn.

'And how did you snare him?' Mock persisted.

'By advertising a reward for news of this Ratsford for whom, it was put about, we were holding a legacy. And before you ask,' Humphrey said presciently, 'we had a dozen or more claimants whose spurious stories we dismissed before Harbottle turned up. They were,' Humphrey chuckled, as if to emphasise the superiority of his lawyer's intellect and its ability to penetrate a fraud, 'easy to discover, General.'

'And Harbottle?'

'Was genuine, I have no doubt. He spoke of satisfactorily corroborative circumstances and seemed more intent upon divulging the information than gaining the reward.' Monck nodded and was about to speak when Humphrey added, 'in fact he came to us, having heard that we were searching for this Ratsford through a third party, a former ship-mate, I think.'

'So he wasn't pulled out of a brothel by the diligent Wragg?' remarked Monck with a relieved grin.

'Goodness me no sir, though Wragg proved a man of uncommon diligence, not to mention discretion, in this delicate matter General Monck.'

'I am glad to hear it, Mr Humphrey, but let us continue to keep the entire matter as quiet as we may, though word of it will rattle like enough…'

'I doubt it, General. The populace frequenting the purlieus of the Highway are either feckless or shifting. Such enquiries are, I understand, common enough: mothers of bastards enquiring for the men who impregnated them, the indebted seeking debtors, cheated seamen after revenge for one reason or another. Indeed the ferment among the crimps and pimps, the whores and the whore-masters, to say nothing of the floating population must tend to an universal amnesia – at least I cannot conceive otherwise if one recalls that this is accompanied by such quantities of gin and other potent liquors. In fact I doubt the matter is recalled even now among those to whom the question was directly addressed but a short while past.'

'I am not so sure. In my experience such things gain an impetus of their own...' Monck fished for the purse and withdrew it, provoking a reaction from Humphrey, who held up his right palm in a gesture of denial.

'Goodness me, no sir; I must draw up your account properly.'

Monck grinned again. 'Of course you must, Mr Humphrey, but this,' and here he laid five sovereigns on the desk, the glint of the gold gleaming in the candle-light, 'this is for Wragg. Do see he receives at least three of them and all five if your sense of honour permits.'

Discomfited, Humphrey gave a thin giggle. 'You jest, General, of course.' Then he recovered his composure. 'Oh, by-the-by, General Monck, Harbottle said that he had come to speak with us because he thought this Ratsford had a wife. Is that why you have an interest in him?'

Monck looked at the lawyer, whose expression wore none of the cunning his words suggested. He leaned towards Humphrey and fixed him in a cold glare. 'The man was a thief,' he said. 'His fatal distemper saves us the bother of hanging him.'

'Ahhh,' responded Humphrey, unconvinced. As Monck folded the affidavit up and placed it inside his purse, Humphrey purred: 'And where shall I send your account, General Monck?'

'To Potheridge, Mr Humphrey, in Devonshire, whither I now go. I give you good day.'

'Well good-night, General Monck, good-night,' Humphreys replied.

And a moment later George Monck was striding happily along the Strand under the brilliant canopy of the stars.

*

Printed in Great Britain
by Amazon

37744378R00101